Andre NORTON

THE JARGOON PARD

A Del Rey Book

BALLANTINE BOOKS • NEW YORK

RLI: VL: 7 & up
IL: 6 & up

A Del Rey Book
Published by Ballantine Books

Library of Congress Catalog Card Number: 83-90024

ISBN 0-345-31192-2

This edition published by arrangement with Atheneum

Manufactured in the United States of America

First Ballantine Books Edition: October 1983

Cover art by Laurence Schwinger

SHAPECHANGER

Back and forth I paced the chamber. I was burning, stifled—

My fingers tore at my clothing, pulling off the cumbersome fabrics and leathers, so that on my body was now only the belt. I looked down at it. The jargoon buckle was blazing—as if it sucked avidly at that heat I felt about me.

The gem dazzled my sight and—

I lifted my head. My position seemed awkward. I could see only at an angle. But—I was on my hands and knees—no! I was—on four padded paws, wearing a body covered in light golden fur. A tail twitched, arose in answer to an involuntary tug of muscle I did not know I possessed. I opened my mouth to cry out, but what issued from my jaws was a heavy half-grunt, half-growl sound.

Contents

Acknowledgments

The author wishes to express her appreciation for the aid rendered on two technical matters connected with this book.

First to Mrs. Merrill Gladstone of the "Rock Pile" who produced a jargoon and also the information concerning the finding of such semiprecious stones, their weight, color and the like.

Second to Mrs. Phyllis Schlemmer, the sensitive, who demonstrated the various forms of tarot and then worked out the proper horoscope tarot reading for Kethan.

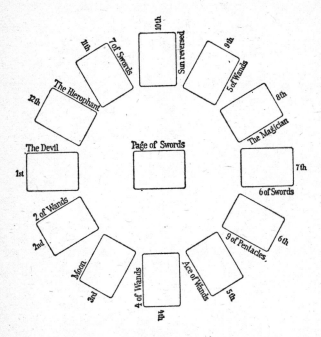

10th
Sun reversed
9th
5 of Wands
11th
7 of Swords
8th
The Magician
12th
The Hierophant
The Devil
7th
6 of Swords
1st
Page of Swords
2 of Wands
6th
9 of Pentacles
2nd
Moon
3rd
4 of Wands
4th
Ace of Wands
5th

Kethan's horoscope tarot reading

The
Jargoon Pard

Of Gunnora's Shrine and What Chanced There in the Year of the Red Boar

Many are the chronicles of Arvon, for that is a land old beyond the imaginings of men, even though those men may be born of the Elder Races and, therefore, long in their own lives. Some tales are near forgotten, so that a songsmith has but bits and patches of them caught in memory. Others are new forged and detailed. For in a land where the Power is known and used, then marvels do follow after, as the long-fleeced sheep of the Dales follow close upon the piping of their shepherd.

There is much in Arvon pertaining to the Seven Lords

and those who ruled before them that is lost, though their judging still lies active in the land. Even those who can wield the Power do not know all, nor ever will.

Who was Gunnora? Was she once a Wise Woman of such stature in the land that after her passing some spoke of her as never having been flesh, but spirit alone? If so— that part of the truth is long befogged. But that Gunnora's influence remains, that all womankind knows, to take heart in. For she is the one whose sign is a sheaf of ripe grain bound together with fruit of the vine ready for the plucking. It is Gunnora's amulet each maid wears, upon which she lays her hand at the moment that she conceives, and that she will hold tightly when the time of childbirth is upon her.

To Gunnora's shrine came those for whom doubtful runes have been cast, that in her sanctuary they may be cured of barrenness, or else have an easier time of child-bearing. And that she has power within the matter of healing, all will testify.

Thus, at Gunnora's shrine, begins the chronicle of Kethan—or if I speak less like a songsmith and more in the common tongue of the land—my own story. Yet the truth of what happened within that shrine at my birthing was a long time hid and held secret. At last only sorcery wrested it forth into the light of day and the full knowledge of men.

It was the custom of the Four Clans—Redmantle, Gold-mantle, Bluemantle and Silvermantle—that inheritance follows the old ways. Thus a man's son does not succeed him in leadership, no, rather the son of his full sister does she bear a boy child. For it be the blood of the women of the Clan that is reckoned the truest by descent. In the House of the Car Do Prawn, she who would provide the heir was the Lady Heroise.

Though her brother, the House Lord, Erach, had wed early, having already a son, Maughus, and a daughter, Thaney (yet an infant in her cradle), Heroise showed no inclination to take any man to her chamber. She was a woman fiercely proud, with a small talent for the Power. As a young maid she had studied with the Wise Women of Garth Howel, bringing one of their number, Ursilla, with her to Car Do Prawn when summoned to return.

The idea was firm in her mind that she should, in time, bear a son to take the chieftain's chair. To the shaping of that son, mind and body, she must bend every care, so that when the day arrived that he was shield-raised by the men-at-arms, and his name shouted to the four corners of the Great Hall, it would be her will that would govern all his actions. And in this project she had the alliance of Ursilla, with all the knowledge of her calling.

Who was the father of the child she carried in the early spring of the Year of the Red Boar no one could name. It was accepted as her right to choose such in temporary alliance only, if that was her wish. Stories were whispered behind hands that her mate was of Ursilla's providing, but it was best not to inquire too deeply into his beginnings lest that be uncovered which would make the coming heir less—or perhaps—more than human. For heir, Heroise was certain, her child would be. And in this Ursilla also gave her assurance.

In the Month of Snowbird, the Lady Heroise and her women, together with Ursilla, traveled to Gunnora's shrine, for the Wise Woman, Ursilla, had cast a foretelling that troubled her. Her uneasiness alarmed Heroise in turn, so that she determined to have all the help she could call upon that the result of all her planning would match her consuming desire. Thus by easy stages, for ragged sweeps of snow still lay upon the ground (though the hint of coming spring was in the air at midday at least), they came to the shrine.

Gunnora has no priestesses nor shrine attendants. Those who seek her out come into a Presence that they may sense but never see. Thus they were met by no one of their own kind. But in the stabling, a little distance from the shrine, were two horses, while in the outer court a man paced

like a great caged cat up and back, up and back, since he
dared not enter the inner chamber, which was Gunnora's
alone.

The stranger glanced at Heroise as she came in, walking
awkwardly because of the clumsy bulk of her swollen body.
Then he turned away quickly, as if he feared that he did
a discourteous thing. So he did not note that Ursilla gave
him a long, measuring glance as they passed him by, and
that a faint frown crossed the Wise Woman's face, as if she
had touched upon the edge of some troubling thought.

But she had no time now for any other save her charge,
for it seemed that the Lady Heroise had miscalculated her
time, and her pains were already upon her. She settled in
one of the small inner rooms, only Ursilla, as a Wise
Woman, attending her, the other women awaiting without.

There was a languorous scent upon the air, as if all the
flowers of late summer bloomed in abundance, and it
seemed to the Lady Heroise that she drifted among the
beds of a great garden. She knew pain, but that was a
far-off thing, which had no tie with her body and meant
nothing. Rather in her now worked a great joy, such as in
her cold and devious mind she had never known before.

Nor was she aware that in a neighboring chamber of the
shrine rested another woman and with her one of the Wise
Women from the neighboring village. She, too, dreamed
joyfully, awaiting a child to fill her arms as love for it
already filled her heart.

Nor were either aware of the storm that gathered, though
the man, who paced and waited, went to the outer doorway
and stared at the black massing of clouds overhead, regarded the clouds anxiously and shivered. It seemed to him
that, though he knew all the humors of nature well and
through many years, the brooding stillness under the dark
roof now stretched over the land was not quite like anything he had seen before. Because of his own nature, he
was alert to forces that were not of the Arvon of men, but
the Arvon of Power. Perhaps now that Power was about

to manifest itself in some fashion that was a threat to all below.

His hands went to his belt, and he ran his fingertips questioningly along it, as if he sought something there that was no longer his to find. But his chin was up, as he eyed the clouds, and what he half-believed might move them so, with a grim defiance. His clothing was plain, a brown sleeveless jerkin over a shirt of forest green. His cloak lay behind within the court. On his feet, the boots of a horseman were dull brown, the breeches above them green.

Yet there was that about him which said he was no field man, nor even chief of some small and unimportant holding, such as his garb suggested. His dark hair was thick and grew in a peak upon his forehead, and his eyes were strange in his weather-browned face—for they were a tawny yellow, like unto the eyes of some great cat. Anyone glancing at him once might well turn to look again, drawn by his air of authority, as if here stood one who answered only to his own will.

Now his lips shaped words, but he did not utter them aloud. His hand rose from his belt to make a small sign in the open air. At that moment there came a great neighing cry from the stable. The stranger turned swiftly—though he could not see around the corner of the building. At a repetition of that cry he darted back, caught up his cloak, and was off toward the horses he had earlier stabled.

He found there the men who had ridden with the party from Car Do Prawn making haste, in view of the storm, to get their own animals into shelter. But the two mounts already there reared and neighed, striking out with front hooves, as do warhorses trained for the fierce battles in the Dales, so that the servingmen and guards swore lustily and fingered their riding quirts, yet dared not push closer.

There were elements of strangeness about these two mounts now prepared to defend their own quarters against any invasion. They were dappled gray and black, the markings not well defined, but so intermingled that perhaps in the wooded countryside, their shading would produce a cover to confuse any who searched for them. Longer of leg than most were they, also, and slimmer of body.

Now they swung their heads toward the man who had come running, and whinnied in combined complaint and greeting. The stranger pushed past the men from the Keep without a word and went to the mounts. At his coming, they stood quiet, only blowing and snorting. Their master passed his hands down the arch of their necks and over their flanks. They made no further sounds as he urged them toward the opposite end of the stabling.

There he put them together within one wide stall and for the first time spoke:

"There will be no trouble, but keep to your own end—" His words were curtly delivered, carrying a tone of order. The commander of Lady Heroise's escort scowled. That such a common-appearing fellow dared speak to him so before his men was an insult, which, in another place, he would have been quick to answer.

However, this was the shrine of Gunnora. Here no man dared test what might happen if blades were drawn— weapons of death bared in a place dedicated to life. Still, the glance he shot after the stranger promised no good at any future meeting.

There was one among the men of Car Do Prawn who continued to stare at the stranger standing between his mounts, a hand lightly laid upon the neck of each as they inclined their narrow heads toward him, one nibbling at his hair. Pergvin had served the Lady Eldris in years gone by, she who had borne the Lord Erach and his sister Heroise. Deep in him memory stirred, yet it was a memory that he would not share with any here. If what he half suspected might indeed be true, what a wild chance of fate had brought this meeting at this day and hour? He wanted mightily to confront the stranger, call him a certain name, see if he made answer. Only there had been an oath sworn in the past after an exiled one went out the Gates of Car Do Prawn never to return.

"Pergvin!" A sharp summons from the commander brought him to the task of helping with their own horses for this was a gale that was like to crush utterly any puny human creature.

So heavy was the rain that they could not see the shrine from the door of the stable, though that building lay only a short distance away. Wind swooped upon them, driving in a lash of icy rain, until they pulled shut the door and barred it. While the stable itself shuddered around them in warning.

The stranger left his horses, went to lay hand upon the door bar. However, Cadoc, the commander, stepped quickly before him, interposing his body between that uplifted hand and the latch.

"Leave well enough alone!" He had to raise his voice to a near shout as the howl of the wind outside deafened them. "Would you let in the wrath of the clouds?"

Again the stranger's fingers dropped to his belt, slipping back and forth, searching. He wore a short sword, but the weapon—closer to a forester's all-purpose tool and clearly no battle arm—was tight sheathed.

Cadoc, in spite of his anger, shifted from one foot to another under the stare the stranger turned upon him. Still he held his ground while the other, after standing so for a long moment, gave way and returned to the far stall where once more he stood between his mounts, a hand on each. But Pergvin, stealing a look when he could, saw that the man's eyes were closed and his lips moved to shape words, which he could not, or dared not, voice aloud. Also, when he watched, Pergvin had an uneasy—nearly shamed—feeling, as if he intruded upon some man who was engaged in that which was very private. He turned away quickly, to seek out his own unhappy fellows who jerked their heads and hunched their shoulders with every blast of wind that struck upon what now seemed a very flimsy shelter.

Their own horses, unlike those of the stranger that now stood quiet, showed signs of panic. So the men needs must work to soothe the beasts. Thus they forgot some of their own fear as they dealt with the animals.

Within the shrine the Lady Heroise was unaware of the fury sweeping beyond the walls. But Ursilla, watching by the Lady, harkened to those gusts and wails, felt the beat of wild nature's force reaching her through the very substance of the ancient building. In her there grew a fear and wonder, for she could not expel from her mind that this was a portent. She longed to be able to use the Power, to perhaps read the meaning behind the fury that now enfolded them. But she dared not distract any of the energy that she kept centered on the Lady Heroise so that their mutual desire be safely accomplished.

In the other chamber, the woman on the couch half stirred out of the drowse Gunnora had sent. She frowned and put out her hands as if to ward off some threat. The Wise Woman, who watched by her, took the hands in hers, willing peace and comfort to return. Not possessed of any great Power was she. Beside that which Ursilla could summon, her talent was the feeble striving of a maid as yet much untutored in the ancient learning. Yet the peace and goodwill in her flowed through her hands and stilled the fear that rose in the half-conscious woman. The dim shadow that had touched her fled.

It was at the height of the storm that the birth cry sounded and from each chamber did it come, one being like to an echo of the other. Ursilla looked down upon the baby she had received into her hands. Her face twisted, her mouth was a wry grimace.

The Lady Heroise's eyes opened, she looked about her as her mind awakened. Her struggle was over, all she had planned and worked for was won.

"Let me look upon my son!" she cried.

When Ursilla hesitated, Heroise pulled herself higher on the couch.

"The baby, what is the matter with the baby?" she demanded.

"Naught—" Ursilla replied slowly. "Save that you have a daughter—"

"Daugh—" It was as if Heroise could not force the whole of that word from her quivering mouth. Her hands grasped so tightly on the covering of the divan that she might be preparing to rend the stout cloth into strips.

"It cannot be! You wrought all the spells the night that —that—" She choked. Her face was a twisted mask of rage. "It was in the reading—that you vowed to me."

"Yes." Ursilla wrapped the birth cloth about the baby. "The Power does not lie; therefore, there must be a way—" Her features set, her eyes stared straight at Heroise. Yet in them there was now no intelligence. It might be that Ursilla's spirit had left her body, sought elsewhere for knowledge she must have.

Heroise, watching her, was tense, very quiet. She did not spare a single glance for the child now whimpering in Ursilla's hold. All her attention was fixed avidly on the Wise Woman. She felt the Power. Enough of her early tutoring remained for her to recognize that Ursilla now wrought some spell of her own. But, though Heroise's tongue uttered no more reproaches, she twisted and tore at the covering with crooked fingers she did not try to still.

Then intelligence came back into Ursilla's eyes. She turned her head a little, pointed with her chin to the wall at their left.

"What you would have lies there. A boy child, born at the same moment as this one you bore—"

Heroise gasped. A way out—the only way out!

"How—" she began.

Ursilla gestured her into silence. Still holding the baby within the crook of her left arm, the Wise Woman faced the wall. Her right hand rose and fell, as with the tip of her finger, she drew signs and symbols on the surface of that barrier. Some of them flared red for an instant, as if a spark of hearth fire glowed in them. Others Heroise could not follow for the swiftness of those gestures.

While she signed so, Ursilla chanted, her voice rising and falling as she recited words, spoke Names. Still never was it louder than a whisper. Yet it carried to Heroise's ears through the rumble of the storm. At the sound of one or two of those Names, she shivered and shrank, yet she did not protest. Greedily she watched, her fierce hunger for what she wanted most alive within her.

Then Ursilla had finished. "It is done," she told Heroise. "I have raised a spell of forgetting. Those within now sleep. When they awake they will have a baby who shall seem to them the rightful one."

"Yes! Do it quickly, quickly!" Heroise urged.

Ursilla was gone, the Lady lay back upon the divan. This she had done—borne an heir for Car Do Prawn. In the years to come—her eyes shone—she—*she* would be mistress there! And with the resources of all the hold land—the lordship—behind her, the heir her creature, and Ursilla to aid her—what else might she not achieve in due time! She laughed aloud as Ursilla returned, a baby wrapped in a birthing cloth once more within her arms.

Coming to Heroise, she held out the child. "Your goodly son, Lady." She used the old formal words of the birthing woman. "Look upon him, name him, that he may have life well set before him."

Heroise took the baby awkwardly. She peered down into his face where eyes dark-lashed were tightly closed, one small fist pressed against his mouth. He had dark hair. Well, that was right. Her own was near the same shade. She pulled away the cloth to inspect the small body critically. Yes, he was properly fashioned, with no mark upon him that could afterward be raised to question his identity.

"He is Kethan," she said swiftly, as if she feared someone to dispute her naming and her owning. "He is my true son, heir to Car Do Prawn, so do I swear before the Power."

Ursilla bowed her head. "I will summon your women," she said. "Once the storm is spent, we had best be on our way."

Heroise looked faintly uneasy. "You said they," she nodded toward the wall, "would never know."

"That is true, for now. But the longer we linger, the more chance may upset our plans, even though I have used mighty spells to further them. She—" Ursilla hesitated. "The one who is the mother yonder, there is something about her that I find strange. She has some of the talent—"

"She will know then!" Heroise clutched the baby to her so tightly that he awoke and gave a little cry, waving his fists in the air as if willing to do battle for his freedom from that grasp.

"She may have talent," Ursilla countered, "but she is not my equal. You know that we can judge another of our kind."

Heroise nodded. "But it is best to be away. Send my women to me—I would they see this baby, know him in the first hour for Kethan, who is mine alone!"

In the other room, the mother stirred. The shade of uneasiness, which had been upon her face earlier, had returned. She shifted her head upon the pillow and opened her eyes. The space of a pointed finger away lay the baby. And over her bent the Wise Woman.

"Aye, m'lady, this be a proper little daughter. She do indeed! Your goodly daughter, Lady. Look upon her, name her, that she may have life well set before her."

The mother gathered the baby into her arms joyfully. "She is Aylinn, my true daughter and that of my Lord. Oh, go and bring him quickly, for now that I am out of Gunnora's care, I feel uneasy. Bring him quickly!"

She held the baby close and crooned lovingly. Aylinn opened her eyes and then her mouth, giving voice to a small cry as if she were not quite sure she found the world entirely pleasant. The woman laughed joyfully.

"Ah, little daughter, welcome are you, thrice, four times welcome. Indeed life shall be better to you than it was to me when I was young. For you have my arms about you and my Lord's strength to guard you—and both our hearts to hold in your two hands!"

Outside the storm began to die. The stranger fought his way out of the stable to meet, at the door of the shrine, the Wise Woman. As he hurried to his wife, he heard a stirring in the other chamber, but it held no interest. Nor did he even watch when, in the morn of the following day, those from Car Do Prawn rode away, their mistress in her horse litter, her son in her arms.

For the three left behind, there was also a faring out some time later. They turned their faces northward to the wilds of the forest, which to them meant home.

Of the Heirship of Kethan and Life in Car Do Prawn

Car Do Prawn is not the greatest of the Keeps that gave allegiance to the Redmantle Overlord, nor the richest. But what it holds within its boundaries is satisfying to look upon. There are orchards of cherry and apple, from which come not only fruit in due season, but also cider, a cherry cordial for which we have no small fame in Arvon. There are also fields of grain, always yielding abundantly at Harvest tide. And there are flocks of sheep and a goodly herd of cattle. Centermost in this smiling and fruitful country sits the Keep itself, and about that a small village. The village lies open under the sun, its cottages possessing sharply gabled roofs, the eaves of which are carved with fanciful shapes. Their walls are all of a light gray stone, the roofs of slate, while those carvings are entwined with runes painted green and gold.

But the Keep itself, while of the same stone, has no such lightsome embellishments. There is always about the Towers a seeming of shadow. It might be that some invisible cloud keeps it so. Within the walls, even in the depths of summer, there abides a chill that none save I ever seemed to note. There I had often the sense that things moved along its very old corridors, in the corners of its shadowed rooms, which had little in common with the ways of mankind.

From the time of my first understanding, my Lady Mother made plain to me that, in the future, I would rule here. But that promise gave me no feeling of pride. Rather, I oftentimes wondered whether any man could claim full sovereignship within such a haunted place. Perhaps my own reticent nature was my protection, for I never spoke to her nor to Ursilla (of whom I was greatly in awe) of those strange and disturbing fancies concerning Car Do Prawn.

Until I reached the age of six, I lived in the Ladies' Tower, where my only companion in age was the Lady Thaney, she who was Lord Erach's daughter and my elder by a year. It had been told me early that our destinies were designed to be one, that when we came to a suitable age, we would be wedded, thus fast locking together the House fate; though at the time this meant little or nothing to me, or perhaps to her.

Thaney was tall for her age, and very knowing, also somewhat sly. I early learned that were we in any mischief together and discovered, the blame would fall wholly upon me. I did not like her or dislike her. I accepted her presence as I did the clothing on my body, the food on my plate.

With her brother Maughus, the matter was far different. He was some six years my elder and dwelt in the Youths' Tower, coming only at intervals to visit his grandam, the Lady Eldris, his mother having died of a fever shortly after Thaney's birth. I say his grandam, though by decent, I was also a grandson. However, the Lady Eldris made plain her preference, and either ignored me, or found fault whenever I was in her sight, so I kept away from her apartments.

Ours was a strange household, though I did not realize that, as it was all I had known. Thus I could believe that all families perhaps lived in the same fashion. Lady Eldris had her own apartments and it was there that Thaney was supposed to stay, though she followed mainly her own will, for her waiting woman was old and stout and more than a little lazy, not keeping as strict a watch upon her ward as custom demanded.

Maughus's visits to their rooms were a signal for me to be on guard. He made very plain when we were ever private together (which I saw, as best I could, was seldom) that he carried ill will for me. He was fiercely proud, possessing much of the same ambition that I knew was inherent in my mother. That he would not be Lord in the Keep after his father caused a bitterness that ate at him even as a child, growing stronger through the years until I was well aware he hated me for what I was, if not for myself.

My mother, the Lady Heroise, and the Wise Woman, Ursilla, had in turn their own chambers, which lay at the top level of the Tower. My mother was much concerned with matters of the household. Whether in the past there had been any clash of wills between her and the Lady Eldris, decided in my mother's favor, I never knew. However, when Lord Erach was absent, it was the Lady Heroise who held Manor Court in the Great Hall and gave the orders. At such times she had me ever beside her, seated on a small stool a little behind the Lord's great chair, which had the red mantle of our clan draped across its back, listening to what judgments she would give. Afterward, she would explain to me the way of this or that decision, whether dictated by custom, or the product of her own reasoning.

That she longed to occupy the seat permanently, I learned by instinct while I was yet a small child. It was as if the qualities that were adjudged by the world to be those of a man had been embodied in her woman's flesh, so she chafed against our customs, decreeing the narrow limits of her own life. In one thing alone she was free, and that was the use of the Power.

Ursilla was the only being within the Keep my mother acknowledged her superior. The Wise Woman's knowledge and talent was, I know, a matter of abiding envy for the Lady Heroise. Though my mother possessed a small talent herself, it was in nowise enough to fit her for the long learning and discipline of spirit that would have made her the equal of her instructress, and that lack she had the intelligence to recognize. But she did not admit in any other thing that she was less than able.

The Lady Heroise lacked the temperament to school her own desires and emotions for any further training in the Other Ways than she had learned in her youth. Even had she not been the vessel to bear the next heir for Car Do Prawn, she would still have been unable to enter into the full training of a sorceress. And to desire so greatly what one cannot obtain because of some lack in one's self is a matter to sour and warp the one who has failed.

If she could not have one kind of Power, then she would excel in another. To this end she now strove with all the force of her ambition.

I have said I was in awe of Ursilla, and I would have gladly avoided her. But, even as my mother enforced upon me her form of training, so did the Wise Woman concern herself equally with my affairs. Though that part of the Power which is wielded by a sorceress is not the same as that which a Warlock or Wizard may summon, still she gave me what learning she deemed useful, carefully pruning such lessons, I realized later, of any material that I could use in an attempt to escape the fate they had set upon me.

It was Ursilla who taught me to read the runes, who set before me carefully selected ancient parchments—mainly those dealing with the history of the Four Clans, with Arvon, and with Car Do Prawn. Had I not had a measure of curiosity about such things, I would have found such tutoring a dull and discouraging time of enforced attention. But I developed a liking for the Chronicles the Wise Woman deemed useful in fashioning my character and learned eagerly.

Arvon itself, I discovered, had not always dreamed away time in this ease of golden days that now seemed endless. In the past (the addition of years was obscure since it seemed that those who wrote the accounts were never interested in reckoning up any strict numbering of seasons), there had been a great struggle that had nigh destroyed all ordered life.

Before that period of chaos, our present domain had not been bordered by the mountains to the south and east, but had spread beyond, reaching east to the legendary sea, also south into territories long since forgotten. However, those of Arvon had always had the talent in lesser and greater degrees, and our Lords and rulers were often also masters of Power. They began to experiment with the force of life itself, creating creatures to serve them—or, in mistaken experiments, ones to slay their enemies horribly. Ambition as strong as that which moved my mother worked in many of them, so that they strove to outdo each other to establish only *their* wills across the land.

They awakened much that should never have been

allowed life—opened Gates into strange and fearful other
dimensions. Then they warred, ravishing much of the
land. Many of the forces they had unleashed were plagues
destroying even some of the Power itself. The disputatious
Lords withdrew as their numbers grew less, returning
here to the home—heart of their own country. Some
came quickly, alarmed and dismayed by manifestations
that they could not control. Others lingered as long as
they might, their roots planted so deeply in their own
holdings that they could hardly face what seemed to them
to be exile. Of these latter, a few never came back to
Arvon.

Perhaps in the Dale land to the south, where another
species of man now lives, they or their descendants still
had a shadow life. But none here knew if that were so.
For, after the last withdrawal, the ways outward from
Arvon were spell-sealed, no one venturing forth again.

Still not all who had retreated were content with their
escape from the results of folly. They continued to challenge their fellows, until the day when the Seven Lords
rose in wrath and might, and there was a final, terrible
confrontation between the ones who chose the path of
struggle and those who wanted only peace and perhaps
forgetfulness.

Many of the Great Ones who had used the Power to
their own wills were thereafter either exiled beyond Gates
that led to other dimensions and times or extinguished
when their will force was utterly reft away. Then their
followers also went into exile under certain bonds of
time.

When I came upon that story in the Chronicles, I asked
of Ursilla whether any of the wanderers had ever returned.
I do not know why that was of importance to me, save
that my imagination was struck by the thought of myself
being so sent out of Arvon to wander hopelessly in an
alien world.

"Some have." She made me a short answer. "But those

are the lesser. The Great Ones will not. It is of no matter now, Kethan. Nor should such concern you, boy. Be glad that you have been born into this time and place."

Her voice to me was always sharp, as if she waited for me to commit some fault she could seize upon. Often, while reading, I would raise my head and find her staring at me with such an intentness that small sins I had reason to answer for were drawn to my mind immediately, and I squirmed upon my stool waiting for her to draw a confession from me by dominating will alone. But this never happened.

What did change was that I reached the age when, by custom, I must go out into the Youths' Tower and there begin the tutorage that would make me a warrior (though for some long years there had been no war except some raiding at intervals from the wild men of the hills). The night before this event, Ursilla and Heroise took me into the inner chamber, which was Ursilla's own shrine, if shrine might be the term given it.

Here the walls were not cloaked with hangings, but unadorned bare stone, having painted on them, in time-dulled colors, signs and runes I could not translate. In the middle of the floor stood a single block of stone as long as a bed a man might lie upon. It was lighted, head and foot, by candles, four of them, as thick as my small boy's arm, set in tall holders of silver much pitted and worn, as if they also had existed for countless years.

Above the table hung a globe from which beamed a silver gleam nigh that of the moon itself. I could see no chain to support it. Rather, it was suspended there invisibly, while about the block, on the floor, was painted a five-pointed star. This glinted so bright and new the brush of its coloring might just have been lifted.

At each star point there stood another tall candle-holder, so that the wax cylinders so supported were on a level with Ursilla's shoulder, well above my own head. The candles at the head and foot of the stone block were red, but those in the points were yellow.

In the corner of the room itself were braziers of the same silver as formed the candlesticks, each putting forth scented smoke, which curled up to the ceiling overhead where it gathered in a blanketing cloud.

Ursilla had put off her usual robe of dull gray, the coif of pleated linen that always wreathed her thin, sharply featured face and hid her hair. Now she stood, arms bare to the shoulders, hair dark, threaded with silver, lying loose over a robe of blue that drew the light of the silver moon overhead, until the fabric rippled with dazzling color.

On her breast lay a great ornament, also of silver, set with moonstones, the gems deeply milky, with about them some of the blue one sees in winter's ice. And this pendant was fashioned in the form of a full moon.

My mother was also differently clad, though she was wont to go richly dressed always. Unlike Ursilla, she did not now appear more finely garbed than usual, but rather more simply. Her robe was orange, owning something of the orange of fire flames, across which her hair hung like a dark cloak. And the ornament she wore was not a moon, but rather an oval fashioned of copper, plain and un-gemmed.

She had led me into the chamber. Now she stood just beyond the edge of the star, her hands tightly gripping my shoulders as I stood before her, almost as if she feared that I might wish to escape. I was so overawed by what I saw that I did not think of what part I might be called upon to play here.

Ursilla moved about the block of stone, and, as she pointed her finger at each of the waiting candles, a small burst of flame answered her gesture as the wicks caught. At last, only the one directly before my mother and me remained unlit.

Now I was urged forward until we both crossed into the floor star. My mother, moving swiftly, caught me up, to lay me prone upon the stone of the table. As she settled me so, I felt suddenly drowsy, unable to move. Nor was I afraid.

The last of the star candles was crowned with flame. Now Ursilla lighted those at my head and feet in the same manner. While above, that waiting cloud of soft gray smoke began to descend. I felt the need to close my eyes. Faint and very far away, I heard a chanting rise. But the words had no meaning as I slipped into sleep.

When I awoke, it was early morning, and I lay in my own bed. I did not even have traces of dreams following me out of that strange sleep. However, the memory of its beginning clung. Again I sensed, young as I was, that I would not be told the meaning of what had happened to me. This was a secret thing about which it was best not to talk.

Commander Cadoc, my uncle, Lord Erach, and the main portion of the forces within the Keep were absent. They had gone with the Harvest gift of wine and grain to the holding of the Redmantle Clan Chief. So it was an older man who came to claim me that morning, one Pergvin whom I had seen many times before, since he was the outrider whenever Lady Eldris chose to move beyond the walls of the Keep.

In appearance, he was a man of middle years, and never a talkative one. Among his fellows he had a well-established place, as he was an expert swordsman and a good rider. But it would seem he had no ambition to climb higher in Erach's service and was content with his life as it was. I was a little wary of him, for the one dark promise that lurked behind the excitement and small triumph of being promoted at last to the Youths' Tower was the knowledge that there I would be largely at the mercy of my cousin Maughus. And since Pergvin was deemed of the Lady Eldris's household, he would also be ready to favor my tormentor.

"Lord Kethan." He spoke formally, sketching a gesture

such as men used to an officer. Then he looked beyond me to where my mother stood, straight-backed, no shade of any emotion on the smooth face, which always bore a youthful glow as if she were still a young maid, with only the glitter of her eyes betraying the mind that was very old indeed in many ways.

"My Lady, Lord Erach has given me governorship over Lord Kethan for the while. All will be well with him—"

She nodded. "That I know, Pergvin. Son—" Now she spoke directly to me. "Bear well what lies now before you, put aside childhood, and reach for all that shall make you more speedily a man."

My excitement had ebbed, my apprehension grew. For in those moments I felt myself far from a man, rather more and more of a child without any security in which I might trust. This Pergvin would take me from the safe cover that had sheltered me all my life, deliver me directly into another world in which Maughus had power and I no defense. That I could stand up to his bullying, I did not believe, having tasted too much of his sly trouble-making during the short visits when I had not been able to escape his company. But that I should ask for any aid, either from that stern person who was my mother, or from this stranger who had come to fetch me, that I would not do. For young as I was, I determined within myself that no one, above all Maughus, must ever guess I felt fear. That was the deepest shame, one I dared not allow myself to sink to.

"You will have a lonely time of it, Lord." Pergvin had not taken me by the hand, I noted thankfully, as if I must be drawn reluctantly to a waiting doom. And when he spoke to me it was with the tone of one addressing an equal in age, not one trying to force awkward conversation with a small boy. "Lord Maughus has gone with the gift party, we shall have the Youths' Tower mainly to ourselves."

I hoped that my relief at that news was not openly

manifest. At least some kind fate had given me a space of time in which to learn a little about this new life without having to be on guard against the spite of my cousin. I longed to ask questions, but my fear of being thought too much a child kept me quiet.

We had crossed the wide courtyard and were near the door of the Tower that was to be my new home when there was a sudden loud barking. A great, spotted hound flashed out of nowhere. To me he looked very large, and, as his lips drew back in a warning snarl, his fangs showed threateningly. But, just as he might have been about to leap at me, he flattened to the ground, his snarls changing to a whining. Though I knew very little of dogs, having seen them only at a distance, this behavior was not natural, of that I was sure. Whining, saliva dripping from his jaws, the dog faced me for a long moment. Then, with a loud cry, he backed away, snapping and snarling, as if he faced some enemy too strong to attack, before he fled, tucking his tail tight against his haunches.

I watched him go in dumb surprise. When he had first appeared I had known a flash of fear. Now this abject terror in the hound's flight was utterly puzzling. Had Pergvin in some way caused that to protect me?

However, when I turned to gaze at my companion, I saw amazement as open as my own mirrored on his face. He studied me oddly, as if, before his eyes, I had somehow grown some monstrous form. Then he shook his head slightly, as if he might be trying so to brush off some confusing fog.

"Now that be a queer happening—" he said slowly, though I believed he spoke his own thought aloud and was not addressing me. "Why should Latchet do so?" He was frowning a little, though the puzzlement was still to be read along with that frown. "Eh, a queer thing that do be. Ah, well, we'd best step out briskly, my Lord. It be close on the nooning and this afternoon we must get you a mount—"

I found the food brought me by Pergvin much plainer than that served at my mother's table, being mainly a round of cold meat, some cheese and bread. But all tasted good, and I left very few crumbs. When I had washed my hands in the table basin, I was willing enough to face my new lessons, which were to begin with riding.

My mother's life had been strictly within the Keep walls, and the one or two times I had been beyond them were to walk through field or garden with one of her women. Neither she nor Ursilla had encouraged or allowed outside exploration. But if I learned to ride, then I, too, could see the wide world, perhaps next year accompanying my uncle on such a journey as Maughus this time shared. So eagerly I followed Pergvin to the stable that afternoon.

He led me down the line of stalls. Horses eyed me over the half doors that kept each in its own place. They tossed their heads, snorted, made ear-piercing noises. Again I was surprised, for when I had watched, from the Tower windows, riders coming and going in the courtyard, I had never been aware of such uneasiness and din.

Men turned about to watch me coming, and several of them hurried to quiet mounts who now reared up and kicked at the wooden walls about them, making an even greater confusion. Then I was aware of Pergvin's hand hard and heavy on my shoulder, as he turned me back toward the outer door.

"Out with you, my Lord," he ordered urgently. "Wait you outside until I come."

I would not run, I told myself, I would walk, though I felt about me a great fog of fear, so that my heart beat faster, and I found myself breathing in short gasps. But walk I did, hoping again to display nothing that these men could see and know to be signs betraying that fear.

Of the Trader Ibycus and the Jargoon Belt He Brought

Pergvin's choice of mount was strange, I thought, but I did not question his actions, for I knew little of the customs of my new life. When he brought forth a slow-moving mare, the weight of years making her step ponderous, I was content enough. Any horse would be a wonder in my eyes at that moment.

Though the mare snorted and pawed the ground once or twice, she stood steadily enough as Pergvin showed me how to mount. However, as I settled in the saddle, she flung up her head and snorted loudly, so that he caught the reins and spoke softly to her, running his hand along the curve of her thick neck as if he had good reason to soothe some fear she held.

She began to sweat and the acid smell was thick in my nostrils. Pergvin led her on, out of the courtyard gate, and into the paddock beyond the Keep where the mounts were exercised. There my lessons began, and I caught eagerly at every word of instruction my tutor uttered, for I found being so mounted was a kind of freedom in itself—promising better to come, even if Pergvin, walking beside me, now kept one hand on the reins that I held awkwardly, while the mare ambled along.

I was disappointed when Pergvin headed once more toward the Keep Gate, hating to exchange the wide outside for the haunted narrow ways within. Just inside the Gate, he halted the mare and swung me down from the saddle, pointing to the door of the Youths' Tower and bidding me await him there, while he led the mare back to the stable.

For the first time then I was aware that there were watchers. Grooms and men-at-arms were unusually numerous in the courtyard. As I crossed, they moved out of my path without looking directly at me. I shivered as I reached the door where I was to wait, for I was not a stupid boy, even if young, and I believed that there had suddenly arisen some barrier about me of which both animals and men were seemingly knowledgeable, though I myself could not see nor sense it. My mind returned to that strange night within Ursilla's chamber. What had been wrought there then that had done this to me?

Now my awe of Ursilla and of my mother was for the first time colored by resentment. For if they had so set me apart from the outer life of the Keep by the art they practiced, then I was surely the loser. I wanted none of of their solicitude even if it might protect me from Maughus's bullying.

As Pergvin neared the stable, the men scattered quickly,

to disappear here and there out of sight, as if they did not wish him to know they had been interested in us. Never before in my life had I felt so alone. But I held my head high, gazing openly around as if I saw nothing of their furtive goings, nor believed that any matter was amiss. Even as I had learned to so protect my thoughts from Ursilla and my mother, so must I wear the same outward shell here, I now believed.

That was my introduction to the man-world of Car Do Prawn. Had it not been for Pergvin always there, quick to offer some unobtrusive advice or aid, I know not what might have become of me. For I learned speedily that all animals had a strong dislike for my company. If I approached the hounds, they first gave tongue as they might on sighting some ordained quarry, then that lessened until they whined, slavered and fled.

I could not mount any horse until Pergvin had soothed it with what I early learned was a dried herb potion he concocted in secret. Even then the creature sweated profusely and shivered while I was on its back.

Yet in the matter of arms, I was not so great a disappointment. Though I was lighter by far of body than my cousin Maughus, still I could make up by a keen eye and the learning of sword skills what I lacked of his strength. With the crossbow, I was a skilled marksman within a year, using a lighter weapon Pergvin produced for me.

It was my delight, along with the sword he had found somewhere in the armory, one more slender of blade and less of weight than the usual, and one that, when I took it up, seemed as if it had been forged just for my service. I asked once if both weapons had been made for Maughus as a young boy, for I did not want to use any of his arms, even if they were now discarded, lest it cause fresh trouble between us. But Pergvin had said no, that these were from an earlier time, fashioned for another youth.

As he told me that, he frowned a little. Though he looked at me as he spoke, yet I had the feeling that he did not really see me at that moment but someone else he had known. So, though I did not often ask questions, I was moved then to do so.

"Who was he, Pergvin? And did you know him?"

For a long moment I thought that he was not going to make me any answer. In truth I had the impression that I had overstepped some permitted bond—just as if I had dared to question Ursilla concerning some part of her forbidden knowledge.

Then Pergvin gave a glance right and left. He might have been checking to see if any were near enough to overhear. However, the Keep was well emptied at that hour, for my uncle had ridden forth on the hunt into the north forest lands. Early it had been learned that such expeditions were not for me, for no horse or hound would stay to their business were I present. Thus was another black mark laid against me openly by Maughus—one I could in no way refute.

"He was a son of the House," Pergvin said reluctantly. "Or rather a halfling son—"

Then he hesitated so long I was moved to spur him on.

"What mean you by halfling son, Pergvin?"

"It was in the long ago when the Lady Eldris was but a young maid. There was a love-spell laid upon her and she answered it—"

He had truly astounded me now. The Lady Eldris was as long lived as all our blood and years counted for little in our aging. But to me, she was a stern forbidding dame with nothing lightsome about her. To think of her drawn by that fabled spell, a love-call, was the same as saying that one fine spring morning the west Tower freed its stones from the earth and danced a planting frolic.

I think Pergvin read my incredulous reception of the confidence in my countenance, for this time his tone was a little drier and sharper.

"All of us were young once, Lord Kethan. There will come doubtless a day when you shall remember and

another be startled at your words. Yes, the Lady Eldris
went as she was called. But it was not a man of our Clans
who laid the spell upon her.

"Those were the days of the Last Struggle, and there
was a gathering of Clans and others who were then our
allies to determine defenses and ploys against the Dark
Lord of Ragaard the Less. Since all who answered the
summons needs must leave their Keeps but lightly de-
fended if they were to join such a gathering, the women
and children were taken to the Clan fortresses for shelter
—those who agreed. For as you know, there were ladies
then who rode in armor and led levies from their own
lands.

"While at the Fortress of the Redmantle, the Lady
Eldris was seen and desired by one of the Wereriders—a
lord among them. It was he who laid the spell that
brought her to his bed. But his spell did not last, and no
real liking came of their meeting on her part. So that in
time she returned to her own people bringing with her
their young son—

"It is said that when she left, her Werelord and his Clan
were elsewhere, for they were always in the midst of the
bitterest fighting, they being what they were born to be.
And, by the time he got note of her going, it was too late
for him to claim her again.

"Her brother, Lord Kardis (he who fell some years
later at the Battle of Thos), gave back freely her Clan
right and laid it also on her son. However, as the boy
grew older he showed the blood of his father the stronger.
At last he went to Gray Towers where he could find
cup-fellows and shield-companions of his own kind. Then
later, when the Seven Lords won peace, those of the
Werefolk were sent into exile, for their blood is ever hot
and they take not easily to a world without war. It was
only a few short seasons ago they returned to Arvon from
far wandering. But I do not think that any old sorrow
binds the Lady Eldris. She later took the Lord Erach's

father to husband and bore both him and your Lady Mother. Thus perhaps time faded all that lay behind. But it is true that her elder son did dwell here in his early youth, and that those weapons were his. However, all this is now a matter best forgot, my Lord."

"Wererider—" I repeated, wishing I dared ask more about that unknown half uncle of mine from the past. Only it was plain that Pergvin would not talk more about him.

There are many strange folk in Arvon. We are not all of one kind or nature. Some are very different indeed when we compare them to ourselves. Of that number not a few are dangerous enough so that those of the Clans avoid them and their territories. There are those totally unlike us as to body and mind, others that mingle within their natures both that which is like unto us and that which is strange beyond our understanding, a third kind that are both different and enemies to our ways.

Yet it is not any physical difference alone that raises barriers between one sort and another, but rather spirits that cannot meet. I have seen the forest people come freely to our sowing feasts, our Harvest festivals. These we welcome, though they are closer to the plant world than to ours. Also I have seen some with the outward seeming of the Clansmen from whom I shrank as if from a blast of winter's strongest cold.

A Wererider, like the forest people, possesses a mixture of inheritance, being sometimes man, sometimes animal. I had come across divers references to such shape-changes in the Chronicles Ursilla had supplied, but at the time I had had little interest in them. Now, because of Pergvin's story, I wished that I had paid more heed to those old hints. For the tale of the Wereson who had used these weapons before me awoke a desire to know more. Had he also in those days felt between him and all others here the same invisible barrier that fed my growing loneliness?

Lonely I was, and turned inward upon my own thoughts

more and more. Had it not been for Pergvin I would have fared even worse. But he companied me under the guise of teaching me a warrior's ways. And, as the seasons passed, he took me on small journeys out from the Keep so that I learned more than just the fields and lands I could see in half a day's riding. I knew though, that in this he was hampered by the rules of my mother, who would never allow me to spend a night away from the Keep.

I was still summoned to the Great Hall whenever court was held there—now sitting behind my uncle, as I had behind my mother. While Lord Erach was just to me after a fashion, he did not extend to me any great kindness. The fact that I could not hunt, that horse and hound hated me, gave him worry, I know. He went as far as to consult with Ursilla on the matter. What answer she made him I never learned. But the meeting led to a greater coolness in him toward me that was a source of unhappiness to me.

Maughus did not bully me openly as he had when I was a child, though he never lost any opportunity to point out my inability to fit neatly into the right pattern of Keep life. Often I found him watching me in such a way as to arouse within me an anger that was partly fear—not truly fear of Maughus himself, but of some formless thing that he might summon in time to my betrayal.

I had passed from boyhood into the time of young manhood when we had an extremely plentiful harvest that overjoyed us all. Yet that was also the Year of the Werewolf, which was an ill sign in every way and which in a measure we dreaded. By rights, this season should have celebrated my wedding to Thaney. Only, under such a sign, Ursilla decided—and Heroise, in spite of her desire to further her plans, backed her—no such uniting could prosper. Thus it was decreed that with the coming of the new year—which lay under the sign of the Horned Cat, a powerful one but such as promised better, the wedding would take place.

Of Thaney I had seen little, since she had gone early to Garth Howel, where the Wise Women gathered, there to learn such sorceries as those of healing and the protection of house and home. It was reported that she showed something of a talent in such matters, which did not, I knew, altogether suit my Lady Mother. Yet, by custom, Heroise could not raise her voice against the furthering of any development of such in her niece.

Maughus was much away also, acting as messenger for his father in various meetings of the Clan or Clans—for all four of the Great Clans were astir.

Arvon itself had passed into a period of unrest which crept upon the land subtly enough. The very names of the years, as they passed, showed that the balance of the Power was a little troubled. For we had behind us such as the Years of the Lamia, the Chimera, the Harpy and the Orc. There were signs that the golden peace of my childhood was fading, though the why of this puzzled all who thought about the matter. And there were embassies sent to the Voices, asking for readings on the future. That this grew cloudier they admitted. Still there was no menace that was openly discernible, upon which men could set their eyes and say—this is what troubles us so.

Pergvin summed the matter up one evening as we sat together over our evening meal.

"It is like the sea tides, this flow and ebb of the Power. When too much of it fills the land, then there is trouble and restlessness." He stared moodily into the tankard of our last year's cider. "It begins so always, too—with the land bearing in great abundance, as if we were being warned to fill up all storage places in preparation for a siege. While in us there gathers an uneasiness of spirit, as if there were a whispering in our ears, urging us to action we do not want to take. So the Shadow comes—as the sea tides—yet not so often—"

"Sea tides?" I caught eagerly upon the two words he had repeated. "Pergvin, have you then *seen* the sea?"

Still he did not raise his eyes to meet mine. Instead he asked a question in turn.

"My Lord, how many years of life think you stretch behind me?"

When I had been young enough to first come under his tutoring, I had thought him old. But, as my own years mounted up, I had guessed him to be of middle life. Age in the people of Arvon was hard to count until they reached near the end of a long, long span of years. Men could die of certain sicknesses, or baneful curses, and in battle. However, natural death and the lessening of vigor, held off a long time from us.

"I do not know," I answered truthfully.

"I was one of those who took the Road of Memory through the Waste in the Dales," he said slowly. "The Great Time of Trouble, I knew, and what followed it. Yes, I saw the sea, for I was born within sound of its never-ceasing waves."

The same awe that I held for Ursilla touched me now. It was as if some hero from the Chronicles had stepped from the parchment rolls to front me. That Pergvin could remember the Exile from the South was such a marvel.

"I remember too much," he said harshly and drank his cider. Such was his air of withdrawal, I dared ask no more.

Then there was an interruption to our evening. A horn cried beyond the Keep Gate, and we recognized its summons as that which announced the arrival of a wandering merchant trader—doubtless come to set up a booth at our Harvest festival. Our welcome to the man who rode within was warm and ready, for traders were widely traveled men who brought with them much knowledge of places our own people seldom if ever saw.

Our visitor was plainly a man of high standing among his fellows, for he did not lead a single packhorse. Instead, he commanded a party with several outriders and a number of goods-carrying animals, among them not only the horses we knew, but several stranger beasts that were long of leg and whose bodies were humped upon the back so that the packs hung lashed on either side of the lump.

By Lord Erach's order the nearer paddock outside the walls was assigned for a camping space, and there the men of the trader's caravan quickly set up a picket line for the beasts, separating the horses from the humped ones, and then tents. Their master was pleased to accept the hospitality of the Keep and a seat at our table for the night meal, with the ladies and their waiting women, eager also to hear any news, occupying their feast chairs.

He was not a tall man, the trader, who introduced himself as one Ibycus (a name that had a new ring, not akin to any we knew). However, though he lacked inches perhaps, he did not lack presence. His manner was easy, with all the polish of a high House, the air of command upon him as surely as it rested on my uncle.

The longer I watched him, the less I believed he was one of our own folk. In spite of his youthful appearance (for in his outward seeming he might as well count not many more years than did Maughus who had not yet returned from his last mission), Ibycus gave a deeper impression of not only age, but of wisdom well controlled. I was led to wonder if he were not perhaps more than trader, perhaps some one of the Wise Ones using his present employment as a useful cloak.

If that was the truth, he was one favorable to us, for there was a lightsome, happy feeling to our dining. The shadow, that always seemed to me to hang within the Keep, was for a time dispelled. We listened to his flow of talk, and he had much to say of the lands he had recently passed through, giving several personal messages from our kin and accounts of how it fared within their holds.

At first I watched him only. Then, as if by chance, I caught sight of Ursilla and the expression that lay on her features. That she had come to meet our guest was a concession on her part, for she seldom visited the Great Hall, keeping to her own chambers. And now—

Yes, there was an uneasiness about her as she watched and listened, as if in this stranger she saw some faint menace. I was sure I saw her fingers move once or twice in a complicated gesture half-hidden by her plate. She might be bringing to bear the seeking of her sorcery to uncover some danger. Yet if that was what she sought, I knew suddenly that she failed. And her failure in turn was a rising source of dismay within her.

It was when the table was cleared that the trader summoned one of his men to bring in a stout chest. After it had been set down before him, he slapped its lid with his open palm, saying, "Wares have I in plenty, my lords and ladies. But the pick of what I carry lies here. With your goodwill, I shall make a show of them."

Eagerly the ladies urged him to do so, their voices rising shriller above the deeper voices of the men who were not backward in such encouragement either. And the chest was opened.

From it Ibycus brought out first a length of cloth, black and much folded. This he spread out and smoothed upon the board before he lifted out divers small bags and boxes, some of silk, some of wood, others of carved bone or crystal. From each he shook its contents, to be flattened out upon the cloth in a display of such wealth I had not believed existed outside some ancient tale of a Firedrake's treasure horde.

There was gold there and moon silver, even the ruddy copper, wrought into very ancient settings for gems. And of the gems—I do not think any of us looking upon that show could have named near the half of them.

We were silent, as if we all at one time together held our breath. Then came cries of astonishment. Also, those

farther away left their seats and crowded closer, to feast
their eyes on all the brilliant glitter. None stretched forth
a hand, a finger, to touch. The display was too overpowering. We must all have had the feeling that it was
too rich for our owning, that we must look, but we could
not hope to possess.

I was one of those who had moved closer, bedazzled
by all that lay there. Then somehow my eyes made a
choice, and I centered my gaze on the article that lay
closest to me.

It was a belt made of golden fur, so sleek and gleaming
that, even among the riches heaped about it, the fur
retained a brilliance, or so it seemed to me. The clasp
was a single large gem—yellow-brown in shade—the like
of which I had never seen. The gem had been wrought
into the likeness of a cat's head. Still, studying the buckle
much closer, I saw that the cat was not intended to
resemble a small, tamed one, but perhaps one that was
akin to the dreaded hunter of the heights, the snow cat—
more deadly a fighter than any other beast we knew.

"This interests you, Lord Kethan?"

At that moment it did not seem strange that Ibycus
addressed me by name, or that he stood beside me. The
others were intent still upon what lay there, and now they
were venturing to touch this piece or that, all talking at
once about their preferences.

But it was the trader himself who took up the belt and
held it out to me.

"A goodly piece of workmanship, my Lord. The clasp
—it is a jargoon, a stone that is of the more common
sort. But it has been most cunningly cut by one who
knows the art well."

"And the skin?" something prompted me to ask.

"The skin—ah, that is of the pard. One sees them
seldom nowadays. They are as fearsome hunters as their
cousins of the snow—though somewhat smaller."

My fingers itched to take the belt from his grasp. At

the same time my will denied that gesture, for I had the belief that if I did I could never relinquish it again. And I had no wealth with which to make it my own.

Ibycus smiled and nodded, as if he had asked some question and had it answered. Then he turned to answer some question Lord Erach called to him.

But I drew back, out of the circle of light about the table, away from the Great Hall itself. For the fierce longing that was in me to possess the belt was such that I was frightened at my own wavering control. Thus I stood in the dark, wondering if it were such a madness as this that forced a man to thievery.

Of the Gift of the Lady Eldris and the Coming of the First Full Moon Thereafter

I sought my own chamber, disturbed by the strong emotion the belt had aroused in me. Though I stretched out upon my narrow bed, I was far from sleep. The moon, which was new, was not strong enough as yet to beam in the windows above my head, so I lay in darkness as I had for many seasons within this same somewhat bare chamber.

The belt! I need only close my eyes to see it in my mind, gleaming as it had in the hall. A curious fancy that the strap had a kind of life of its own haunted me.

I wanted fiercely to run my hands along the furred surface, to take into my hold the carved head, gaze deeply at the jewel of its fashioning, as if I could read therein some foretelling of the future, as the Wise Ones do.

At length I could lie still no longer, so distraught did my craving for that length of fur render me. I arose and went to the window, resting my arms upon the sill, for the opening was set so high that the sill was at shoulder height for me. There I lingered, looking out into the night.

The Youths' Tower was the northernmost of the Keep and the window faced that direction. I could make out dimly the fields and orchards that stretched outward— the village lay southward. Beyond, the forest began, a wood wall between us and the high hills, which held so much that instinct taught us to avoid.

For the forces of Arvon that had wrought disaster in the past had, in the last reckoning, fled back into the hills and forests. Barriers of the unseen Power, as strong as the concentrated will of the Wise Ones and the Seven Lords had been able to set, restrained them there. No man knew now if any of those we considered the enemy still lingered, or whether they had opened other gates between worlds, those that they knew so well to manipulate, leaving Arvon.

Some of their servants, the lesser ones, were still a menace. But it was part of the nature of those that they were tied to certain portions of the land and did not often stray from their accustomed "runs." Thus, for the main part, they could be avoided. And, of those, some were in a way an added defense to our own heartland, prowling about to keep out any man from south of the Dales who might venture to explore in our northward direction.

The Dales! I remembered what Pergvin had told me— that he was one who had taken the Road of Memory, the Road of Sorrows, followed by the exiles who had withdrawn during the dark days into Arvon. Those who dwelt there now were not of our race, being lesser, in that they had not the Power, barbarians only a few generations away from utter chaos. They were short-lived, too, seeming to last but a day or so of our time before they matured, then died of that age, which had set a deadly finger upon them from their birth. We had naught to do with them.

Dark was the night, though the stars were brilliant overhead. They glittered as did the gems Ibycus had displayed. From the north came a wind that reached fingers within my window, chilling my bare flesh. Yet I did not go back to my bed and huddle into the coverings there.

Rather, I found my head well up, my nostrils expanded to drink in the wind, as if it carried some message. There was a faint excitement, born deep within me that I had never felt before. The night's very darkness drew me, beckoned. I had a queer flash of thought—how would it feel to run bare of body through the grass, to splash into a stream unheedingly—to—?

The excitement died as swiftly as it had come. I shivered now. The dark promised ill instead of joy. Drawing back from the window, I settled upon my bed. Of a sudden, the sleep, which had eluded me, descended. I yawned, my eyes burned, as if I had been too long without rest. Stretching out, I slept.

There was a dream—from it, I started awake. My heart was racing as if I had been running at top speed, my body was slick with my own sweat, and yet the chamber held no great warmth. The first gray light of predawn made a showing in the narrow slit of window. I sat up—what had I dreamed?

I could remember nothing, had carried out of sleep no hint of what had so—so— Was it fear that had moved me or some other fierce emotion? Even that I could not now answer. To return to sleep was impossible.

Moving quietly, I washed in the waiting basin. The

water was chill, but not unduly cold. I began to dress, still fighting a blocked memory for some hint as to what I had dreamed. For though I could not recall it, the doubt lay heavy on my mind. That dream *was* of great importance—I *must*—

However, as I moved about the normal task of dressing, the urgency also began to fade, so that when I went softly out of my small chamber, none of it remained. I felt slightly foolish, as if I had hurried to meet someone who had no intention of fronting me.

When I reached the middle court, I discovered another before me. The trader Ibycus stood watching the door from which I came. He was smiling a little. At sight of me, he nodded. Then I was sure that this encounter had been planned, though for what purpose I could not guess.

"A fine morning, early though it be, Lord Kethan." His voice came low but clear.

I was a little at a loss, being sure he had a purpose in meeting me, yet unable to guess what that purpose might be. His air was that of one awaiting a longtime friend, though he greeted me with formal address. In turn, I felt that about him, which made me swear he was no trader, but deserving of the fullest respect, as much as the High Lord of my own Clan, or one of like position.

"A fine morning, Lord." I found my tongue at last.

"Lord?" He put his head a little to one side, his eyes very bright as he surveyed me. I might be now some trade object he had to value. "I am a trader, not the master of a Keep."

Something within me was stubbornly certain that, while he might not be master of any holding within Arvon, neither was he trader only. Thus I met his gaze squarely, awaiting enlightenment.

Ibycus raised his hand to finger his chin. Upon the forefinger he wore a large ring. The stone, which formed its setting, was unlike those among his treasure, being dull, without any brilliance or life. It could well be only a bit chipped off the nearest field rock. In color the oval was a sere gray; the setting that held it was, I thought, silver. Yet if so, that metal had been allowed to tarnish, which also made me wonder. For the ring was indeed a poor-looking thing for the master of such riches to choose for his own wearing.

"Lord Kethan"—he still smiled—"it seems you are one with eyes in your head."

I flushed. Had he so easily read my thoughts? A talent for such discernment was what the greater of the Masters were rumored to possess. Suddenly he thrust out his hand toward me, not to grasp mine, but so that the ring was near on a level before my eyes.

"What do you see?" he asked.

I ran my tongue tip over my lips. What he wanted of me I could not guess, but that there was some deeper meaning in this encounter I was now very certain. Obediently, I gazed upon the ring.

There was a kind of shimmer across the stone. The dull surface appeared to move as might the surface of a pond when one tosses in a stone, rippling—

Then—

I think I must have exclaimed aloud, my surprise was so great. For an instant or two I had seen the head of a cat thereon, a snow cat, its fangs exposed in a snarl of warning! So much life was in that picture I did not believe it was any carving resembling the one of the belt buckle.

"What do you see?" So imperative was the order in his repeated question that I answered with the truth.

"I—I saw the head of a snow cat!"

Now Ibycus held his hand before his own eyes, peered intently into what was once more the dull gray of the stone. He nodded abruptly.

"Well enough, Lord Kethan, well enough."

"Well enough for you perhaps," I was embolded to say then. "But what is the meaning—"

The trader did not allow me to finish the question. "In

due time, my young Lord, all shall be made plain. Just as it is plain to me now why I came to Car Do Prawn. I make mysteries you think?" He laughed. "When you were a small lad did you not learn your runes by beginning with the simplest combinations? Would you have been able to read any Chronicle then put into your hands without such preparation?"

I shook my head. I wanted to be angry at his usage of me, indeed at his hinting and his mysteries. However, there was that about him which kept my tongue discreetly silent.

"This I leave with you as a thought to hold in mind, Lord Kethan—be guided by what you desire most, not the demands others shall try to lay upon you. Even I cannot read some runes. They must be revealed properly in due time; and sometimes time marches but slowly. You shall be given a gift—cherish it."

With that he turned away abruptly before I could speak, though I stood, mouth half-open, like a fish gasping above the water of its safe pool. Nor did it seem that I might follow him to demand an explanation of his words, for something outside myself kept me where I was and silent.

He went directly to the Ladies' Tower. Apparently he was awaited there, for the door swung open at his first knock. I remained where he had left me, chewing over the words of his speech.

I did not have any private meeting with Ibycus again. By nightfall he had gathered his train of men and pack animals to depart from the Keep. That he had made some sales of his wares was certain. My mother and the Lady Eldris had kept him long while they decided over what they might afford. But I believed that not much of his treasure remained behind when he rode out. And I deeply regretted the belt.

However, I told myself repeatedly, I could never have hoped to purchase it. In addition, there were none within

Car Do Prawn to whom I would appeal to aid me in acquiring such a thing. Though I might be Lord Erach's acknowledged heir, yet I had no purse into which I could dip.

Three days later, came the day of my birth anniversary. When I had lived with the Lady Heroise and Ursilla, this had not been made an occasion for any feasting. Rather, it was celebrated as a solemn time when Ursilla had worked some spell or other, my mother assisting her, aiming at me the force of their Power, always, as they explained, to strengthen and protect my small self.

But, after I moved to the Youths' Tower, if they still carried on such a ceremonious marking of the day, they no longer required my presence during it. So the date became like any other, save that, by record, I was deemed a year older, and more would be demanded of me in wisdom and strength.

Therefore, I was surprised when there came a message that the Lady Eldris wanted my attendance, the reason being given that it was that date. The night before, Thaney had returned, escorted by Maughus and a suitable train of waiting women and outriders. As I put on the best and newest of my feast tabards (the one stitched with the device of my heritage), I wondered if they planned this day to make some formal announcement of our coming marriage.

It was late afternoon when I crossed the courtyard to the other Tower. Within, the light was dim, so already the waiting maid who admitted me held in one hand a lamp that burned well, emitting a scented vapor. Following her, I climbed the first flight of the old, worn steps to the apartments wherein my grandam had her rulership, though memory almost sent me higher, toward the portion that had once been my home.

Within the presence chamber, there was no daylight at all, for the walls were close hung with tapestries, the colors of their patterns muted. Yet here or there, the light of one of the lamps would catch the face of an embroidered figure or grotesque beast and bring such to life. Lamps there were in plenty, others hanging from chains suspended from aloft.

These were all ablaze, giving forth heat as well as scented vapor, so that the room, after I had been within it but a moment or two, was stifling. I longed to pull aside one of the hangings and find a window that could be flung open for fresh air.

The Lady Eldris sat in a high-backed chair between two of the pillar lamps. There was no silver in the thick, dark braids that swept below her waist when she arose and that were interwoven with threads of soft gold, interset with green and pale yellow stones. She, too, wore the tabard of ceremony, enclosing her body stiffly from throat to hip. A single great green stone, like a third eye to watch me, rested in the middle of her forehead.

Like Pergvin, she had aged little, her appearance was that of one in early middle years. And, while she did not wear my mother's openly displayed arrogance and need for dominance, she had authority in her person, underlying her every gesture.

I made my manners carefully, going to my knees and putting my lips briefly to the hand she held out to me—a hand chill to the touch in spite of the concentrated heat of the chamber. Though my head was bent in courtesy, I was keenly aware that she eyed me up and down, not with the satisfaction she always turned in Maughus's direction, but with the aloof and faintly hostile withdrawal she had ever shown me.

"Greetings to you, Kethan—" she said, making the words by her tone merely words, without warmth and welcome.

"Good fortune, sun bright and lasting to you, my Lady." I gave the proper answer.

"Stand up, boy. Let us see what the years have made of you!" Now there was a hint of testiness in her voice.

It meant she was constrained to this meeting for some reason and she did not propose to make it an easy one for either of us.

Arise I did. Now I saw that, though two of her waiting women hovered in the background, neither my mother nor Ursilla were present. But another advanced at the Lady Eldris's beckoning. That this was Thaney, I had no doubt.

She was the Lady Eldris over again, as her grandam might have been those untold years ago when the Wererider had set a love-spell to ensorcell her. As tall as I she stood, the stiff formal folds of her tabard and robe hiding but still hinting at the curves of the body beneath, a body ripe and ready for marriage. She had the same dark hair of her grandmother, but looped and arranged into a great coil on the back of her head, secured in place with gem-headed pins and combs.

Her face was as I remembered it, regular of feature, but there was a petulant twist about a mouth that appeared proportionately too small, and already a faint frown line between her dark brows. She was not smiling, but rather looked sulky, as if she clearly desired to be elsewhere at this moment.

I knew the action custom demanded, though reluctance to carry that out grew in me. However, having no choice, I reached forward to clasp her hands, draw her close enough to kiss her cheek. I could feel the tension of her body and understood well that there was no response from her, except perhaps a quickening of dislike.

"Very pretty!" My betrothed had said nothing, not even my name as a greeting. It was the Lady Eldris who made the comment.

"Well, girl." She spoke directly to Thaney. "You will not do so ill after all. He is presentable—"

With that she paid me no compliment. I was keenly aware of a mutual contempt they might well have shouted aloud. Still I was firm in my resolve that neither of them would I allow to know that. Betrothal—solemn as that ceremony might be—was not marriage. To that thought I clung now, for there moved in me the knowledge that never could I take Thaney to wife. There must be some way to gain my freedom.

The Lady Eldris waited for no answer from either Thaney or me. Instead, her hands dropped to her lap to pluck at the strings of a silken bag resting there. Those loosed, she drew out—

The pard belt!

Again the moment I saw it, I experienced the same fierce and rending need to make it mine, the need I had somewhat forgotten since the time I had last seen it.

"A goodly token, girl, for your future. This forms a tightly closed circle, such a circle as your marriage must be. Give it—with your vow—to your future lord!"

Thaney did not at once reach for the length of fur, dangling from the hand her grandam held out to her. Did she fear if she did complete the gesture the Lady Eldris demanded of her she would be irrevocably pledged to a future she disliked? Apparently, she dared not completely defy the order, however.

Taking the belt at last, she turned to me, her voice as sullen in tone as her mouth looked while she uttered those words:

"My Lord, accept from me this symbol of our future unity."

I had only half an ear for her words. The belt was all that mattered. Yet I restrained myself, so I did not actually snatch it from her hold. I had enough presence of mind to thank her and the Lady Eldris.

Thaney did not even nod as my words died into a somewhat embarrassed silence. I saw that the Lady Eldris was smiling derisively.

"See that you guard it well, Kethan," she said. "It is a very great treasure, indeed it is. Now you may go. We have fulfilled the bargain and I am weary—"

Her dismissal was so abrupt as to make me angry. But such words and actions were only a scratch across my pride. In truth, I was well pleased to be out of the hot, perfumed room, my treasure looped about my arm. As I returned to my own quarters, I ran my fingers continually across the fur, reveling in touching such silky warmth. Also, I did not put it away in my coffer as I laid aside my festival clothing, but had the overpowering fancy to fasten it about my bare waist under my jerkin. To me there was no strangeness in what I did. There it felt right. It seemed needful that I wear it so.

That night when I sought my bed I did not lay it aside, but kept it on. Again, it was a night when I could not sleep. Gazing from the window into the dark was not enough. Rather, as the full moon rose, I knew that I must be out—free—away from this pile of time-pitted stone.

Though I had never done so before, I pulled on breeches and boots, taking time for neither shirt nor jerkin. I slipped out of the Tower, through the Gate that in this time of peace had no sentry on duty. Once in the open, I began to run. There was a headiness and wildness in me that possessed by body, urged me on and on.

I crossed fields to enter the screen of bushes forming the outer fringe of the woodlands. There I kept along the banks of a stream, so that the moon-dappled waters sang at my side, until I at last reached a glade where there was the full silver of the moon and a pool reflecting it. There I ripped off my clothing and leaped into the shallow water, cupping it in my hands and splashing it up over me. The belt formed a darker line about my body, while the gem of the pard's head took fire from the moon in a way I had never seen any gem burn before. It blazed up, more and more. I was caught in a fiery cloud. There was nothing now but the wildness alive in me, the flashing of the pard's snarling head before my dazzled eyes.

Of the Warning from Ursilla and the Cloud over Arvon

When I awoke with the coming of morning, birds twittered in the trees above me. The fire of the moon had left the pool, though a dwindling silver disk still rode in the west. I blinked and blinked again, bemused at what lay about me, for in my mind there was a memory—a memory of wild, exultant life enclosed within the night. I had seen more, heard more, scented more of a strange world, vividly alive, than I ever had in my life before. This was the freedom that something long buried inside me craved. To return to the Keep was like forcing myself back into a cage, yet I had no alternative.

Some instinct also warned me that, were my night's adventure known, I would be prevented from repeating it. I must regain my own chamber unseen. I sat up quickly, reached for the breeches and boots, which lay an arm's distance away, to pull them over my dew-moist skin. The belt about me now was just a belt. Even the gem buckle appeared duller, as if half-consumed by the fire that had blazed under the moon's touch. Still I ran my hands lovingly along the furred loop where it cinched about my middle.

The hour was still very early. I hoped to reach my chamber before there was any stir in the Keep. Again, some caution I did not understand led me to take a way along which there was cover. Thus I skulked, in the fashion of a scout approaching some enemy camp. I reached the Gate and slipped through to run for the Tower door. In doing so, I must pass the entrance of the Tower wherein the ladies dwelt. Someone moved out from the arch's shadow there to front me.

Ursilla!

There was no avoiding a meeting with her. She had turned to face me and her hand beckoned, drawing me to the arched doorway as she retreated into that more private place.

When she did not speak, I fidgeted from foot to foot. Then she pointed to the belt where it showed against my skin, only half-concealed since I was not wearing a jerkin.

"Where got you that?" Her voice was a harsh whisper, meant to compel the truth from me.

Again by instinct my hands were at my middle, cupping over the gemmed buckle. I had a queer feeling that I was threatened. Also, I was angry with myself for being so submissive to her, Wise Woman or not.

"It was a gift," I returned with scant courtesy. "The Lady Eldris and Thaney gave it into my hands as a betrothal pledge."

Ursilla's features sharpened, her lips pulled away a little from her teeth. Just so had I seen one of the great hounds snarl in soundless rage.

"Give it to me!" Her fingers stretched out, curling to resemble talons, as if she would tear it from my body. "Give it to me!"

By the very force of her emotion, she released me from the spell of obedience she had cast.

"No!" I denied her with a single word. Then turned and ran, unmindful now of anyone sighting me. It was not until I reached my own chamber and stood there, panting, that I regained control over the panic that had taken me out of Ursilla's reach. I dropped down on the edge of my narrow bed and tried to sort out my own mixture of emotions to learn, if I could, what had brought me racing here like a frightened child.

The sense of freedom with which I had awakened had gone. In its place arose a frustration, mingled with fear. I was in a cage—and Ursilla threatened to keep me therein. She would see that I did not repeat this night. I was aware of that as if it were written in flaming runes upon the wall before me. The belt!

I unhooked the buckle, held the gem head on a level with my eyes, examined it closely. Yes, in the day, it was dimmer. But there was no way Ursilla would get this from me—no way! It was truly mine in a manner that nothing had ever belonged to me before. I had known it instantly when I first saw it laid out among Ibycus's treasures. That the belt had been used by the Lady Eldris for her own purposes, intended to bind me to those purposes, mattered nothing. All that did was that I could now fasten it about my body. This I again did, checking the buckle well to be sure it was surely closed.

Ursilla might be mistress of potent spells, but get this from me she could not. I do not know why I was so certain of that fact, only that I was.

However, I was not to escape the Wise Woman so

easily. It was midafternoon when the message came. I
had been at swordplay with Pergvin and had won from
that expert a certain measure of approbation. Since he
was always more critical than commending, I felt new
triumph. Perhaps that sense of being more alive, which
I believed the belt afforded me, would now work to give
me prestige among my fellows. So I was in a good-
humored mood, which was not even dashed by a per-
emptory summons to my mother's bower.

As I crossed the courtyard I was sure that this must
be some ploy of Ursilla's and that within the influence of
the rooms where she had her own center of Power, it
behooved me to go very warily indeed. Only I was no
longer a small boy to be ordered about; at this moment,
I felt all man grown, the master of my own destiny
and life.

There was no sign of either the Lady Eldris or Thaney
as I passed by their chambers, ascending to the floor
where my mother ruled, with Ursilla ever at her shoulder.
The cloying scents were gone as I climbed. Also, the room
into which the waiting maid ushered me had no enwrap-
ment of tapestry about its walls. Rather, it possessed
uncovered windows through which came the light of day
and the smell of the drying hay on the fields below.

Still there was richness here, also. My mother's chair-
of-state was as highbacked, as well cushioned, with its
red mantle of House draped across it, as that of the
Lady Eldris. And, in place of the tapestries, the harsh
stone of the walls framed strips of parchment on which
were painted uncanny-looking birds and beasts quite unlike those I had ever seen, the colors brightly laid on to
make their scales, feathers, claws, horns and the like,
brilliant and as near glittering as gems.

My mother sat with a lap table before her on which
was spread just another such painted strip, where, within
dark outlines, she was pointing a brush with care, filling
it with small flecks of scarlet, and then, taking up a

second brush, outlining each of these with a speck or two of gilding. She did not raise her head at my entrance, nor bid me any welcome.

I was used of old to such treatment, since she would not take her eyes from her labor until she had completed the particular portion of the picture she worked upon. That she was alone surprised me, for I expected Ursilla to be present, yet of the Wise Woman there was no sign.

The Lady Heroise placed the two brushes in a narrow tray upon her table and pushed it away from her. She surveyed me, coldly and critically.

"You are a fool!" She spoke at last.

Since that reception also I had had before, it raised no resentment in me, only a desire to have her come more quickly to the point and explain in just what fashion I was foolish.

"You have let them bring you to heel as if you were any hound from my Lord's pack," she continued coldly. "Why I should have a son so wit-lacking that he cannot even see when he is being leashed to another's purpose—" She shrugged. "What is done—at least it can be undone."

Still I waited. It pleased her to approach the subject in this involved fashion. When I was a child such maneuvers had some influence on me, so that I grew uneasy the longer she was inclined not to state my fault directly. Now, after years of this, I was able to curb any emotion her words aroused until she reached the heart of the matter.

"The Lady Eldris is—" she began and then hesitated. I had early learned that between her and her mother there was no love and very little liking, though when they met, their formal manners were well controlled, and they displayed the united front that custom demanded of them. That my mother had replaced the Lady Eldris as mistress here was sure and established, but I had never, through the years, caught any hint that this state of affairs caused any resentment. It was rather as if her mother had been content to relinquish the cares and duties of chatelaine to her daughter.

"You have been caught in her net," the Lady Heroise now stated firmly. "If you do not break that influence early—" Again she hesitated. Then, at length, she apparently decided upon the blunt truth.

"The belt is cursed."

That she believed what she said, I had no doubt. But that Ursilla had put that thought into her mind I was also certain.

"In what manner?" For the first time I broke silence with that question.

"It is a thing of the Wererace. Ursilla knew it for that when first she saw it. That the Lady Eldris must also have known it is our misfortune. For she saw in it a chance to get what has long been her will."

"That being?" I asked again. In my early dealings with my mother, I had been very manageable. Now for the first time in my life, I could think my own thoughts and be myself. Perhaps this was because it was less than a full day's time since I had tasted freedom such as I had never known before.

"To bring Maughus to the heirship." Again my mother stated simply what must long have lain at the core of a silent struggle of will. "She gives to you this cursed thing in such a manner that it cannot be refused, setting upon it the symbol of betrothal. Already the belt has begun its work— Where ran you last night and in what form, Kethan?" She leaned forward, and her eyes seemed to blaze as they stared at me, in a lesser blaze perhaps, but not unlike the glitter the moon had drawn from my belt.

"I slept beside a woodland stream. I ran nowhere. And I am no shape-changer, my Lady."

This was the result of Ursilla's meddling. At that moment, however, another face flashed into my mind, that of the shrewd, pleasant, trader. What had he said to me at our private meeting? "Be guided by what you most desire and not the demands others would lay upon you. You shall be given a gift, cherish it."

Now I added my answer, a question:

"How knew the Lady Eldris that her gift carried this Power?"

There was more than annoyance in my mother's face. There was a flash of pure anger.

"From the trader, how else? Ursilla scented Power in him. He can only be one of those set to stir up mischief and strife. In other days there were such, traveling among our people, striving to influence them this way or that. Ursilla has read the stars. They are not well positioned for Car Do Prawn, perhaps even for this land."

"You say that the Lady Eldris favors Maughus, that I know. But custom is custom. She cannot pass over the fact that I was born your son, thus am heir." I was feeling my way cautiously, again as might a scout in forbidden territory, but here I must deal with words and not patches of shielding shadow among fields.

"Fool!" My mother arose to her feet, giving an impatient shove to the table that sent one paintpot to smash upon the stone. She paid no attention to the breakage. "A shape-changer is always vulnerable. Unless he is a trained Were, he has no control over such changes. Do you think that any within Car Do Prawn would accept your lordship if they knew that was your failing? It was tried here once before. There was an heir true born before Erach, of a different father. He was half Were, and when that was known, his mother, all within these walls, exiled him. You are not even half Were. Wear the cursed belt and you will not be able to control shape-changing. One moment a man—the next an animal! Do you think Thaney—any maid would wed with you? You would be hunted out from these walls. And—the longer you cling to that thing of horror—the deeper will become its hold on you! Give it to me!"

She held out her hand in imperious command.

What she had said, she believed. But the fact remained, I did not. To me this was a brew of Ursilla's making. I had not forgotten her gaze turned upon the trader, the way her fingers had covertly moved as if she tried to spin some spell against him. I had no liking for the Wise Woman; in fact, during the past days, since my meeting with Ibycus, my feeling toward her had moved from awe and uneasiness close to detestation.

"This is Ursilla's bidding," I said slowly.

My mother's hand dropped to her side. Her tongue tip showed between her lips, moved back and forth as if licking away something that lay there and was not to her liking. Her eyes had narrowed, and now her face was devoid of expression.

"You will obey me!"

I did not know until that moment that I possessed the strength to set my will against hers. And, as I found that possible, a frail wisp of the exultation I had known upon my waking brushed my mind. What did I care about their intrigues?

When I made no answer the Lady Heroise suddenly smiled, as if she had controlled the anger she had let me see.

"Very well." The change in her tone was so abrupt that I was unable to adjust to it at once and was caught off guard. "Cling to your toy, child. You shall learn and when you do, pray that it is not too late and you have not lost all through your stupidity. Get out of my sight until you learn your duty and come back to it in the proper spirit."

She seated herself composedly, drew her lap table once more into position, reached for her brush. It was plain that to her I no longer existed. But she had accepted a small appearance of victory on my part that heretofore would have been unthinkable.

I left the Tower with much to consider. Was Ursilla's story the truth? Had the trader for some hidden purpose given the Lady Eldris a tool to use against me? Opposed to all my mother said, what did I have as arguments? The impression the trader had made upon me, the sense of complete rightness and confidence the belt had given me and the memory of a short part of the night free under the moon. All small, almost shadowy things, still they held me back now from believing that my mother—or Ursilla—might be totally right.

I knew that the Lady Eldris bore me no goodwill, and doubtless Thaney agreed with her. Who within the pile of Car Do Prawn, I wondered then, did have any friendship for me? To my mother and Ursilla, I was to be a tool. I had realized that since the time I had first knowledge. Lord Erach showed me no favor, only a kind of tolerance. Maughus, I was sure, hated me. Who else—Pergvin? Only perhaps.

And to him I could go with no questions about the belt. I knew what his reaction would be—give it up so I might not be more unpopular than I now was. As I recrossed the courtyard, I felt very much alone in that hour. Again in my room I unlaced my jerkin, pulled loose my shirt, and sought the clasp of the pard head.

It would not yield to my fingering!

I worked more and more furiously, striving to loose the buckle. It remained as stubbornly closed as if it had never opened before. In growing panic, I now believed that it was a thing of Power and perhaps it *had* come to possess me.

Staggering to the window, I leaned against the sill, drinking in cool air. My heart labored and my hands shook a little as I rested them on the stone, fighting for control. I—must—not—let—myself—open the gate to fear. Calmly, rationally, I must find the catch, loose this—

I rubbed my sweating fingers on my breeches to dry them, made them move slowly, not convulsively tear at the buckle. One pushed—thus—

The pard's head released its grip, the belt loosed,

would have looped free to fall to the floor, had I not caught it.

I held the strap up into the full light of the window, angry with myself. See how they could play upon me— make me believe their tales. A catch sticks a little and I am condemned to wear a curse about me! "Fool," my mother had named me. Looking upon the belt I knew I was not that. I would be the greater fool if I let myself be ruled by their desires.

The wonder the belt had held for me from my first sighting flooded back. It was a precious thing! There was no harm in it. Instead, when I cherished it, I was nearer the free man I dreamed of being. If Ursilla would chain me again, she must have this. And she would not!

I clasped it about my waist with determination, hid fur and gem once again with shirt and jerkin. I was lacing the last when Pergvin came with a word from my Lord that I was to attend him in the Great Hall at once.

There was truly a gathering of authority awaiting me there. Not that I had any standing or could voice an opinion, but, as my Lord's acknowledged heir, I must be present at his decisions. Cadoc, who was his Commander and Marshal, Hergil, a quiet, older man whose passion was the keeping of the records and who was reputed to know much of those who practiced the Were Power, were there. Hergil had been on a month-long absence from the Keep. But so unobtrusive a person was he that one did not miss his presence much. Neither did he speak often. But, need any reference be made to some event of the past, and it was to Hergil one applied for confirmation.

Maughus was very much to the fore. The years between us seemed to grow more instead of fewer as the seasons slipped by. Where he used to torment and belittle me, he was now wont to ignore me entirely. That I did not mind. Now he sat hard by his father, a goblet in his hand. This he turned around and around in his fingers as if admiring the time-blurred design embossed upon its sides.

I slipped into a place beside Hergil (none of them acknowledged my presence), subdued as always by the atmosphere of age and austerity that formed my impressions of the place.

"It is true then"—Erach spoke heavily, as if whatever news he must make plain to the rest of us was not of a favorable kind—"that there will be a muster of forces. We stand with The High Lord Aidan as does Bluemantle and Gold."

"But Silver?" pressed Cadoc, as my uncle lapsed into silence.

"No man knows. There has been coming and going between the Keeps of the western marches and the Inner Lands."

"Silver ever had a liking for alliance with the Voices of the Heights," Hergil commented. "It was they who held the Hawk's Claw for nigh half a year in the days before we took the Road of Memory out of the Dales. Their blood is half of the Oldest Ones under the moon."

"But who meddles?" demanded Maughus suddenly. "I have been messenger to some twenty Keeps. I have ventured clear to the Whiteflow. Everywhere men are uneasy. They have taken now to riding armed when abroad. Yet there is no reported foray of the Wild Ones from the Higher Land, no war horn has sounded."

I thought of Pergvin's talk of how tides of trouble ebbed and flowed in Arvon, and that it was near time for our time of peace to be overset. But not to know the enemy for what he was—that was to loose upon us an unease greater than certainty might produce.

"We do not know," his father replied then. "Yet such is our heritage that we can sense a storm ahead. It is said that the Voices read the star charts and so can foretell. If this they have done now, they have sent forth no warnings. It may well be that one of the Gates shall open and some terror long ago expelled through it return, strengthened and armed, to confront us."

"There is this," Hergil said in his quiet voice. Low though his tone was, we all turned our eyes to him. "There has been a great warring throughout our world. The Dales have battled ruthless invaders and, after a long term of years, driven them forth again. Overseas those of our cousinhood have also been embroiled in a struggle that has left them near beaten into the ground. This war they won, but in the winning, they made such an effort with the Power that for generations they will not be able to summon much to their service again.

"Thus our element of defense has been drained bit by bit, both from the new peoples who are not of our blood and from those who are like unto us. Who knows if such a draining has not weakened the safeguards of our world so that those beyond a Gate, or Gates, sense—or know— that this be the hour to move again?"

"Pleasant hearing!" commented my uncle. "But perhaps in the gloom lies bitter truth. For ourselves we can only try that we not be caught utterly defenseless. Therefore, let us live each hour as those who must prepare against a siege. Then, if disaster breaks, we shall be as ready as we can be without clearer knowledge. To each then a task—"

He began to lay out duties and labors for us all. Thus, in the stirring of some menace we could not put name to, I half-forgot my own private misgivings.

Of Maughus's Plot and the Opening of My Own Eyes

By my uncle's desire I dealt with the harvesting of our outer fields to the north. There I labored with our field men, not only checking in the loads upon the wains sent to the granaries about the Keep, but also aiding to pitch the bound sheafs upon those same wains. For with the feeling of pressure that had fallen upon us during those days, there was no division of rank, we worked hard together to make sure that we would be, as Lord Erach had promised, well prepared for any siege.

All other of our Clan Keeps might have been likewise

employed, for no messengers came during those weeks. Nor were there now any lightsome plans for a Harvest fair such as had been our way in other years. It seemed better that each man remain in the safety of his own roof place and not go riding abroad farther than the limits of his own fields.

Each night I stumbled to my bed so spent of body, so drugged of mind by the long labors of that day that I had no thought of aught except a need for sleep before the dawn horn would arouse us in the morning for further efforts. I continued to wear the belt, but in those days, it was no more to me than any other article of clothing. Nor did I hear more from either my mother or Ursilla.

They were busied also. The brewing of our cordials, the preserving of fruit, the baking of the hard journey bread (which could be kept without spoiling for long periods of time) lay in their hands. Even the children of the village hunted down nut trees on the edge of the forest, disputing with the woodland creatures for the spoil of that hard-shelled harvest, dragging home bags of kernels that could be picked from their tough coverings, ground into meal, and used to season and add taste to bread.

The days, then the weeks passed, and time came once more to the full moon. Our labors were slackening. The greater part of all our land could produce in the way of food was now well stored. We had had perfect weather for that garnering—no days of rain—not even the over-hang of a threatening cloud. Almost we could believe that the Power itself was extending this favor to us.

However, at times I heard the field men grumble. Or, when they straightened their backs for a moment's rest, they looked about them with eyes that were not content, but questioned more and more. Their portion was too easy this year and they mistrusted that ease, fearing such might forerun some great difficulty to come.

On the eve of the first full moon, I rode the last wain

back from the final field, my bones aching as if I had
never known any rest for my body. There was no laughing,
nor playing of rude jokes among my crew as had always
been the portion of men released from hard but successful
labor in other harvest times. I noted that, though our head
reaper had woven the last stalks into the rude likeness of
the Harvest Maid and the men toasted her in the cider
sent to the field, yet they did so without joy, but as if
this, too, was a duty that must be followed.

Nor did the Keep stand cheering as our wain trundled
in, the Harvest Maid impaled on a pitchfork to top our
load, though a semblance of the proper ceremonies existed
in that those of the Keep had turned out to see us come
into the courtyard. And my uncle gave the signal for a
second toasting to the Maid.

I recognized the girl who handed the tankard to me.
She served in my mother's quarters upon occasion. Only
now she gave me no smile, nor any word or greeting, but
went mumfaced.

With my back set to the wall of the Youths' Tower for
support, my arm so tired that I could hardly force it to
rise at my will, I brought the tankard to my lips and
drank thirstily. This year even the cider had a bitterness
to it that lingered on the tongue, so I did not finish my
portion.

I was so spent after I had stumbled up the stairs to my
chamber that I made no move to drop my clothing or
wash my body in the water that stood waiting. Instead, I
straightway fell upon my bed and closed my eyes. And
I must have instantly fallen into a deep and dreamless
sleep, for of that night, I remembered no more.

My awaking was slow. The sun painted a bright, glittering patch on the floor that hurt my eyes. The mighty
ache that had been in my back the night before, now
seemed to pulse within my skull. I raised my head, and
the stone walls about me wavered, a bitter sickness
flooded in my throat.

By will alone I lurched across the chamber to where the tall ewer of water stood. My hands trembled so I had to use both to raise it, and I splashed more liquid to the floor than into the basin beside it. But I scooped up some of what gathered there and dipped my face into it.

The chill of the water on my skin brought me out of the daze that had cloaked me. I was able to master my heaving stomach a little. That I had some illness—no! My mind moved sluggishly, but I was remembering the bitter taste of the cider I had drunk the night before. And she who had brought me the potion was under Ursilla's bidding.

Now I became aware that the stained and rumpled shirt I had worn to bed was no longer laced, but flapped loosely about me, baring my body and—the belt!

My hands flew to assure me with touch that the report of my eyes was the truth, that it had not been reft from me. However, that theft had been attempted was my strong suspicion. The drink had been drugged. Ursilla knew well the lore of herbs, both helpful and harmful. Such learning was a necessity for any Wise Woman. Why she had not been able to accomplish her purpose while I lay helpless I could not understand. Nor could I confront her, or my mother, with mere suspicion.

But this experience proved that I must begin to mistrust what lay about me. My stubborn conviction that I would not surrender the belt, no matter what scheming might lie behind the Lady Eldris's gift, was only strengthened by these suspicions. I would not be forced, nor plundered, if I could help it.

While I stripped and bathed in what water was left, brought forth fresh clothing, my mind was busy. It came to me that the moon's phases might have something to do with Ursilla's actions. I wished I knew more of shape-changing. Perhaps if I approached Hergil— Dare I? I hesitated to take any action that might reveal a weakness Maughus could seize upon.

Were the Lady Eldris and Thaney only waiting for me now to betray myself? I shrugged on a clean shirt, the linen of its folds pleasantly scented with the herbs used to battle those inroads of damp and mildew that haunted the Keep walls, drew its lacings tight, once more hiding my belt.

Tonight again there was a full moon. I had answered to the wild excitement the belt had engendered the last time only once—on the first night of such a moon. But, since Ursilla's drugs had prevented me last night from any experience, could it be that the second night might answer as well?

I must know and I could not trust the word of any— even Hergil. Certainly not that of my mother or Ursilla. Therefore, this day I would walk with care, eat and drink with greater concern—which would be easy enough. During the Harvest there were no formal meals within the Great Hall, men were given cakes of journey bread, cheese and dried meat directly from the kitchen when they so called for it. By the temper shown last night, I did not believe that there would be much feasting this day. And, even if such be served, I could fill myself with fruit and the like, avoiding aught that might be meddled with.

When I issued forth from my chamber, it was near midmorning, so long had that drug kept me in thrall. The courtyard, in contrast to the activity of the past few weeks, was almost slumberous. I could hear voices from the stables, but no one moved in the open. Though my stomach had earlier troubled me, now I felt a great hunger and made my way to the buttery hatch where one could obtain a serving of bread and cheese upon demand.

As I rapped upon the sill one of the cook boys bobbed into sight. His own chin was sticky and he was licking crumbs from his lips as he eyed me, flushed of face, as if I had caught him out in some petty pilfering.

"Your wish, Lord?" he squeaked and near choked in

the process from some ill-chewed lump he had swallowed in far too great a hurry.

"Bread, cheese—" I told him shortly.

"Cider also?"

I shook my head. "What I have said, no more."

Perhaps my words were a little too forceful, for he looked surprised as he went. I was annoyed by my small self-betrayal. Care and care—that I must take now.

He reappeared with a course napkin for a server. In that was a thick portion of bread that had been raggedly slit open and a lump of cheese pushed in. Since the bread was still warm enough to melt the cheese a fraction, I thought I could accept it as trustworthy.

I gave him thanks and, with the napkin in hand, I straightway made for the gate and so came out into the open of the day. The sun blazed overhead with hardly a trace of cloud to be sighted. At this hour the dew was well sucked away from grass and bush, and the mown fields were dusty brown, almost withered looking. I turned my back upon them and went along an ancient path of moss-grown blocks into the garden where herbs and flowers were grown, both for their scents and their healing virtues.

However, here too was company. I heard the higher voices of women, saw three who moved among the late-season roses, harvesting those full-blown blooms that would be rendered into cordials or sugared for sweet-meats. Having seen the maids before they saw me, I slipped into another path, bordered by high-growing berry bushes, now nearly stripped of their fruit burdens.

It was the sound of my own name that made me pause. Though I had no intent of listening to the chatter of those busied with their rose culling, yet to hear oneself spoken of is bait few, if any, can resist.

"It is true—they sent old Malkin to the Youths' Tower in the night—to the Lord Kethan's chamber. She came shuffling back, sniffling as if she feared to have her ears

boxed near off her head. I would not wish to run errands
for the Wise Woman. She—"

"Best bridle your tongue, Hulda! That one has eyes and
ears everywhere!" There was a stern warning in the
rebuke.

"I reckon there are eyes enough on our young Lady.
She has sulked for days and her temper rises with the sun
and does not set with it. Yesterday she threw her mirror
at Berthold and cracked it side to side—"

I heard a sound like a breath sucked forebodingly.
"That is an uncanny thing."

"So the Lady Eldris told her," retorted she who had
reported the happening. "Also our Lady pointed out that
mirrors are not commonly come by, and there may be no
more traders this season from whom Thaney can get
another. Then Lord Maughus came in and they put on
smooth faces and sent all from the room that they might
talk in private."

"Yes. That was when Malkin was on the stairs so long.
I say she is one of the ears you spoke of."

"If she can hear through door and wall, her ears are
far better than most. She is so old I wonder that she can
still creep around."

"Have you ever thought—" And now the voice asking
the question dropped to a tone hardly above a whisper,
yet it came clearly to me. "Have you ever thought that
Malkin might be—different?"

"What mean you?"

"She serves the Wise Woman, but no other. I heard
old Dame Xenia once say that Malkin came with the
Wise Woman and that, even in the days that are longer
ago than any of us are now old, Malkin looked the same,
like a worn old shadow barely able to creep about. You
know she never comes into our solar, nor has she ever
spoken, that I heard tell of, unless someone asks her
some direct question. There is a strangeness about those
eyes of hers, too.

"Though she keeps them most times cast down in a way that veils them from anyone who looks upon her, yet, I tell you, when she goes into the dark, she never takes up candle or lamp to light her way, but walks straightly as if dark still be light to her."

"The Wise Woman seems to trust her. I wonder why she was to seek out the young Lord. Ralf saw her on the stairs, and then he watched her lift the latch of the Lord's chamber. Nor did he hear any sound of voice within as if she brought some message. He wanted to learn more but his lord summoned him straightway and he did not have a chance—"

"Peeking, prying—you and Ralf—would you get the Wise Woman to turn her eyes upon *you*, Hulda? You are very unwise if you chance that!"

"Yes. And do not tell *us* your tales, either! I have no wish to gain either her notice or her ill will! It is enough that we must live with the changes of spirit our young Lady shows, or the sometime full angers of the Lady Eldris. Let those who serve above have their own worries. Let me see the baskets—ah, we have enough for the first drying. And do you both watch your tongues and think no more of what Malkin does or does not do in the night!"

I heard the swish of their skirts as they moved from me. But what they had said fully confirmed my suspicions that it was Ursilla's hand and mind that lay behind my night of unconsciousness. Well, her servant had not gotten what she had been sent for, though I could not count that as any triumph on my part. As I found a bench at the far end of the garden, one sheltered by two walls of shrubs, I chewed my bread and cheese, more mindful of my thoughts than the food I swallowed.

Upon one thing I was determined, that come nightfall this eve, I would not be any prisoner of Ursilla's. Should I stay apart from the Keep, here in the open? The memory of that wondrous night upon my first putting on the belt was enough to make me long for another. Yet perhaps, were I missing, my mother might well summon out a force to hunt me down. It would be better that aught I did be done secretly. Though she might have set them to watch and spy upon my coming and going.

The sun did not reach in to me here, and there was a drowsy contentment in the garden that began to lull me. Fat bees, about *their* harvesting with the same vigor as we had shown these past weeks, blundered heavily laden from flower to flower, and birds sang. It was very hard here and now to believe in intrigue and danger.

Slowly, I became aware of something else, that my own senses seemed heightened in a way I had never before noted. When I looked about me colors were brighter, the outlines of plants and flowers sharper, more distinct. The scents caught by my nostrils were richer, my hearing keener. I do not know why I was so sure that this was so, I accepted it as the truth.

There grew in me a need to be one with the growth about me. I dropped from the bench to kneel upon the grass, run my fingertips among its blades as if I lovingly combed the fur of some giant placid beast slumberously well content. I bent my head to sniff at the faint, delicate perfume of some tiny flowers that hung bell-fashion from a stem as thin as a thread, to tremble a little in the air displaced by my movement. The wonder of what was happening filled me until I forgot all that threatened, was content to just be in this place at this hour.

Such a moment could not last. As it faded slowly, the old doubts and lacks of my life returned stronger than ever. In this place, I now felt like one who disturbed peace, a brash intruder, so I left.

There was not a feasting, but a dining together that night. I sat in my place looking from face to face, alert to any glance, any change of countenance that might gain me fuller knowledge. There was laughter and much giving of toasts, thanks brimming for the bountiful Harvest.

However, all this surface clatter rang shallow, and those gathered here seemed feverishly bent on making a clamor, perhaps to drown out their own thoughts.

I ate with care, sparingly. When I replied to toasts, I was thankful for the solid metal of the goblet that did not reveal that I touched lip only and did not drink. Also, I contrived to pour away the liquid surreptitiously into an urn, filled with flowering branches, that luckily was placed behind my seat.

Ursilla did not show herself. But my mother fronted the Lady Eldris across the board, and Thaney sat among the unwed maids at their own table after the custom. I was conscious that Maughus watched me from time to time. But his regard I did not fear at this moment as much as I did some hidden act. For I believed that his dislike was so open any move he might ever make toward my discomfiture would be delivered without need of subtlety before the faces of all.

Our dining broke up early. There was little heart for the games and singing. Throughout the meal, Lord Erach, though present in person, seemed otherwhere in thought, though now and then he spoke low voiced to Hergil. And he wore a frown that deepened with every such exchange.

I was growing impatient. To be by myself, to attempt once more to elude all the Keep and those it contained, to hunt out the freedom I had savored, the need worked within me until it seemed that I could no longer control it. So I slipped away, heading for my chamber since I knew better than to seek the outside when any there might watch my going.

Only—when I deemed that it be time that I could try to leave and I set hand upon the latch—I discovered it had been made fast outside. Then indeed I cursed myself for a fool! How easy a way to bring me under control—yet I had not foreseen it! Had Ursilla somehow ensorcelled me from afar so I had overlooked so simple a thing and taken no precautions?

Back and forth I paced the chamber. There was no cool breeze through the window. Rather now the walls about me radiated heat as the moon arose and its silver beamed outside. I was burning, stifled—

My fingers tore at my clothing, pulling off the cumbersome fabrics and leathers, so that on my body was now only the belt. I looked down at it. The jargoon buckle was blazing—as if it sucked avidly at that heat I felt about me, used such to build up an inner energy.

The gem dazzled my sight and—

I lifted my head. My position seemed awkward. I could see only at an angle. But—I was on my hands and knees—no! I was—on four padded paws, wearing a body covered in light golden fur. A tail twitched, arose in answer to an involuntary tug of muscle I did not know I possessed. I opened my mouth to cry out, but what issued from my jaws was a heavy half-grunt, half-growl sound.

Against the far wall rested the polished shield that was not only made for battle, but that served also as a mirror. I moved toward it and saw reflected in its center—a pard!

Yet there was no fear, no panic in me following the first moment or two. Rather I lifted my head high and knew a triumph and a glory in this body. Why did men speak so evilly of shape-changing? In their ignorance they did not realize what might come to him who so tasted knowledge that was not of his own species—his limited species—

I gloried in my muscles, in the quick sinuosity of my movements as I prowled back and forth. And I was so caught in the wonder of my change that I did not hear the lifting of the latch. It was only when the light of a lamp banished the moonlight that I whirled about, snarling.

Just in time, I sighted the bared steel of a sword, knew that was what Maughus waited for, that I should attack him. However, though I might wear a new shape, my own mind was still in command. I would not play my cousin's game so easily.

He was not alone. Darkly cloaked, the hood half slipping from her head, Thaney stood behind his shoulder. Her face was a wry mask of disgust.

"Slay him!" Her hoarse whisper rasped in my ears.

Maughus shook his head. "No, he must reveal himself as what he is—I am too well known for my dislike of him. I will have no man say my sword drips his blood because I would have his heritage. But you see the truth of it, sister. He is a shape-changer. We need only say that and men, in their present state of dreading all that may be manifestations of the Dark, will get rid of him for us."

He moved back, still holding the sword at the ready. The door slammed. I heard once more some bar drop across, prisoning me within.

Of the Wild Hunt
and My Flight Therefrom

For a moment the beast was uppermost in me. I leaped for the door, crashing against it with bruising force. Whatever bar Maughus had set held stoutly. When I heard my own snarl, the sound put a curb to the animal part. What my cousin intended for me I could not guess, but that it would be a peril great enough to endanger perhaps even my life, I believed.

No longer did I delight in my new body. I wanted out of it, back into the familiar shape that was truly mine. Yet I knew no spell, nor trick of ensorcellment, which

would win that for me. Bitterly I realized how right
Ursilla had been, my mother had been, in distrusting the
belt. My mother had named me "fool." Now, in my
desperate plight, I laid a far harder name upon myself.

What had happened was only too plain. Somehow—
perhaps through the trader Ibycus—the Lady Eldris had
learned the secret of the belt and made sure that it would
be put into my hands. Thus she could well remove me
from the path of her favorite. Because I knew only too
well that what Maughus had said moments ago was the
truth—a shape-changer had no good name among those
of the Clans. Such a one was alien, one with the forest
people, the halfling bloods that the wholly human never
quite trusted.

With those of the Keep people so worked upon already
by the cloud of suspicion that had crept slowly to poison
their peace, they would treat me as they had Lady
Eldris's halfling son in the long ago—drive me into exile.
But my lot would not be even as good as his, for I had
no Werekin to seek out, no other shelter awaiting me.

The belt—I lowered my head, looked at my furred
body. Yes, beast form though I might wear, the belt was
also still about me. I could not distinguish its fur well
because it matched my own present hide. But the jargoon
head shone bright and clear. Suppose I could rid myself
of that binding? Would I regain man form so?

However, though I hooked at the fastening with the
claws of one paw, jerked and pulled at the buckle, it
remained fast closed. The window? Dared I leap from the
window, find a place to hide until moonset? That much
lore I had learned from the Chronicles—that the full
moon largely controlled such changes.

I reared up on my hind legs, rested my paws upon the
sill, crowded head and shoulders forward that I might
stare down. My chamber lay in the second story of the
Tower, the drop below was sheer and without a break.
I was not yet used enough to my new body to attempt

such a leap; and, as I stood so supported within the window frame, I heard a small sound from the direction of the chamber door.

It required but an instant to drop to four feet again, pad across to listen. Had I really heard the stealthy withdrawal of the bar that held me prisoner? I was not sure.

If the barrier was now gone, who had taken it? Maughus wishing to entice me out for his dark purpose? Or did I have some friend here who wished to upset my cousin's plan?

I lifted a forepaw and extended the claws, catching them in the crack between door and wall. Slowly, and noiselessly, I levered. The door responded, moving toward me. It was unfastened. Knowing that, I paused to listen. For I was sure that the hearing possessed by my new shape was superior to that of any man. Just as the air I drew into my wide nostrils held scents I had never known before.

There was no sound from without. I heard not the slightest hint of breathing of anyone set to attack when I came forth. A choice was before me—remain where I was and await the fruit of Maughus's malice, or escape —if escape I could—and meet him later on my own terms.

The scales inclined in favor of the latter decision. Again I pawed at the door, this time perhaps applying too much strength, for it swung widely open. The light without did not seem overly dim to me. Again the pard's heritage was mine. In my mind I had a plan of what I must do. There was only one person within this stone pile who might now give me aid (not for my sake but because of her own plans)—Ursilla! Learned in the old knowledge, she would know what could be done to rid me of this shape, or at least hold me in safety until the hour of natural change came. Then—I must in turn yield to her demands and let her have the cursed belt. With that gone,

Maughus could prove nothing, do nothing—

I slipped noiselessly out of the chamber. The smell of man was strong and with it another odor that brought an involuntary snarl to wrinkle my feline muzzle—hound. However, I could see no one, hear no one. Whoever had released me from the trap my own quarters had provided had not lingered. Pergvin? Yet how would he have known —unless Maughus had talked freely of what he suspected and planned to do.

The stairs were before me. Softly, I skulked down them. Before me was another portal, this one also barred, but with the bar resting on my side. I rose, my paws braced against the door, set my muzzle under the edge of the bar, pushed awkwardly.

At first the length of metal resisted, but then it began to move, with a grating sound that seemed thunder-loud in my ears. I paused to listen—more than a little suspicious now. What if Maughus had set up this whole venture to tempt me into the open where he could make public my change before I could reach Ursilla? Yet what choice did I have? To hide in my chamber tamely and wait to be unmasked was something my nature would not allow me to do.

Finally, the bar thudded back far enough to release the door. I gave it a strong push and so won out into the open. There I slunk into the nearest shadow to listen and to sniff.

Horse—hound—man—strong odors, but ones I knew even when in my own body. With them were a myriad of new scents I could not put name to. In spite of my determination to be utterly done with the belt and all it meant, there was some excitement, the feeling of freedom, rising within me. I had to force myself to control those impulses, to realize there was now only one possible freedom—to be released from the belt and what it had laid upon me.

I surveyed the Ladies' Tower. The lower door would

be night-barred on the inner side— Then I thought of
Thaney. If she had issued forth secretly from there, might
she not have left it unlatched, ready for her return? However, upon that I could not depend. There was the outer
wall of the Keep that stood on the far side. Were I to
gain that, it could well follow that, from the higher
surface, I could leap to the window of my mother's apart-
ment, which fronted in that direction. At the moment, I
could see no other way.

Yet to gain the top of the wall I must go through the
outer guardroom, up stairs meant to aid defenders to
reach the parapet in times of siege. Now there was an
unnatural quiet about the courtyard itself that I found
disturbing.

To pass the way I must go, I needs must skirt both
the stable and the run where the hunting hounds were
kenneled. Knowing how strong animal odors were to me,
I could not but believe that both horses and hounds
would scent in turn the pard who slunk past. All I needed
to bring about discovery would be such a sudden clamor
in the night.

I could not remain where I was, though. So, my belly
fur brushing the stones, I began a stealthy swing toward
my chosen goal. I was never to reach even the edge of
the stable.

A clamor of hound cries broke the still of the night as
if ripping apart the sky itself. Into the moonlight burst
the foremost of the pack that my uncle boasted would be
ready to face even a snow cat at bay. They continued to
give tongue, yet they did not close in upon me. But the
fear and anger born of their charge filled me, driving out
the man, giving full freedom to the beast.

I leaped, claws extended. The hounds yelped, crowded
back. Now the horses within the stable must have caught
my scent, for they seemed to go mad, their wild whinnies
rising. Men were shouting, pouring into the courtyard.
A crossbow bolt whistled by me.

The hounds were between me and the Gate. If I did not win past them, I would be shot. There were not enough shadows to give me cover and the hounds would nose me out of any hiding place. The largest, the pack leader, Fearfang, was between me now and the Youths' Tower.

He alone of the bristling, snarling dogs seemed prepared to carry the fight to me. He paced, his eyes shining redly in the limited light, his lips lifted in a continuous snarl, though he uttered no sound. The animal in me knew that, while the others were made prudent by fear, this hound wanted only battle.

I gathered my feet under me. My tail twitched. Then I jumped, my bound lifting me over the pacing threat of the hound. Nor did I halt then, but went through the Gate in great leaps, heading for the open, which to the beast side of me was the only promise of escape.

The hounds, heartened by my retreat, gave tongue loudly. I knew that Fearfang must be in the lead. Also, there was more shouting now. Over my head arched a flaming fire arrow, to strike in the stubble of a field and provide a torch that already was lighting the chaff about it.

The arrow was my answer as to whether or not I had entered what was meant to be a trap. Someone had loosed the hounds, had prepared the arrow and others like it now streaking through the sky to strike about me. Not only was I betrayed as a shape-changer, but, in addition, I would be hunted. Were I to die during such a hunt, he who planned the action could plead that he had taken me for truly being the wild animal whose guise I wore. And I knew in my heart that Maughus meant to make completely sure of me.

For an interval I fled blindly, my only thought to keep ahead of hounds and hunters. That there would be hunters I had no doubt at all now. Then once more my mind brought under control the frightened beast. It was needful that I get away from those who hunted me, yes, find some shelter where I could wait until the day destroyed my ensorcellment. But that I could not do by purposeless flight.

I had never ridden on any hunt. The peculiar reaction of both mounts and hounds had kept me from learning the skill that was considered so much a part of a man's training. Thus I had no knowledge to guide me now— unless—

Unless I allowed, deliberately allowed, full rise to the part of me that was pard, not man! Dared I do so? I was reluctant, yet the fear of death may present one with bitter but unescapable choices. I tried now to submerge the man in the animal, discovering it frighteningly easy to do.

What followed then was as if I was a distant spectator of my own actions. The queer separation within me was hard to define for anyone who had not experienced it. Yet it existed, and, I think, did save me from what Maughus intended.

My speed had well outstripped any riders, though I could hear their cries, even the sound of a rallying horn. If any fire arrows now fell, they landed well behind, just as I was slipping from the fields.

I dug claws into soft bark and climbed into the first of the more massive trees. But that in itself was no refuge. The hounds need only gather below and they would have me trapped, to be held for the arrival of their masters. Many of the trees were giants—their lower limbs wide enough for me to pace cautiously. From the first such I made a desperate leap to the next, catching hold of a second limb, then scrambling to walk and climb for a second airborne advance.

Four trees did I so use to break my trail. However, there was no further way offered from the fifth. All I could do was jump as wide as possible, landing in brush that broke under my weight, to my discomfiture.

The strip of woodland, while narrow, ran far to the

north, reaching into the hill region usually avoided by the Clan people. That it had other inhabitants, I well knew, and some of them could be summoned by my hunters to give news of my going. Others were such as I had no wish to meet either as a beast or man. If I might only find someplace to lie up until dawn I was sure that my escape would be assured. Beyond that point I did not now try to look.

The clamor of the hounds had grown fainter. Perhaps they were baffled by my expedient of taking to the trees. They might well be doing sentry duty under the one I had first climbed. I did not run wildly now, but slowed to a steady pace.

From my right came the sound of running water, perhaps the same stream that had drawn me on my first venture with the belt. Water, too, could be used to cover my trail. I veered off from the direction I had been traveling and came out upon the stream bank. Here the moon shone fully. To my cat's eyes, all was near and clear as it might be for a man at midday.

I pushed into the water, involuntarily hissing as it washed about my legs nigh shoulder-high, disliking the sensation of wet fur. But I trotted on against its current upstream. I do not know how far I so journeyed before I reached a sprawl of rocks with many wide crevices that appealed to the animal part of me as adequate for concealment. The moon was riding down the sky now. In so much I had won. I need only stay here until the morning and—

However, all my wariness, my stratagems, had been for naught. There was a flash of wings in the air over me. Then the same wings were buffeting my head, my shoulders. Pain lanced my body, as a great hawk used beak and talons on my back just above my loins. I threw myself down to roll upon the ground, beat up at the bird, still so shaken by the sudden attack that I did not know how to counter successfully.

Though I lashed out, squalling as any infuriated cat might, the hawk had achieved its purpose. I watched it rise, my last frenzied leap falling far short as the bird spiraled upward. In its talons hung the belt, swinging limply, its buckle still clasped, but the hide of its making clawed and torn in two.

I crouched upon the stone. The gashes the bird had left in my back during its ruthless attack smarted with pain. Worse was the fear that, with the belt torn so from my possession, I had been exiled to beast form. If I only knew more of shape-changing! And why had the hawk—?

The bird could not have been any servant of Maughus's. No normal predator could have been trained for such a purpose. No—the creature was either one of the unknown and to be feared aliens of the forest—or— A sudden thought made me growl. Ursilla?

I had no idea of the width of the Wise Woman's knowledge. But I had a hearty respect for what she might do. That she might accomplish such an act as this could not be denied. Now I was not even sure that the bird had been a true hawk. It was well known that those dealing with the Power could summon divers strange servants. While such an act had never occurred in the past when I had lived with Ursilla, I dared not judge this to be outside her range of talent.

If Ursilla had the belt! Sorely shaken and not a little afraid, I looked about me, and, choosing the largest of the crevices, I crept inside.

Catlike, I licked the moisture from my fur, strove to put healing tongue to the scratches my attacker had left. But few of them could I reach. Then I lay full length, my head resting on my forepaws. The night and the chase had been long, my body ached for sleep. Rest— I could no longer deny it.

I think I half-expected to wake and find myself ringed with the hunters. But I hoped that I would rouse in the form of a man. When the sun reached well into my hiding place and I opened my eyes, it was to know the full truth. I was still a pard. Knowing that, I realized fear to the full, the fear that had first touched me when I had seen the bird wing off with the torn belt. I was trapped in this form without the key to shape-changing.

Also, I awoke with the deep hunger of the animal, the absolute need to fill an aching belly. Once more, if I were to survive, I must let instinct overbear human reason. That instinct led me to the streamside.

Fish swam there. Sighting them, saliva filled my mouth, drooled a little from between my jaws. I hunched down, poised a paw. A swift movement, then a fish flopped beside me, leaving me absurdly pleased at the result of my untried skill. My fangs snapped and I gulped down mouthfuls, hardly tasting what I ate.

The stream dwellers had fled, there would be no more caught here. I padded along past the rocks, made another try—and missed. But the third landed me an unwary catch twice the size of the first. Having finished it off, I sat up on my haunches to look around.

Where I might now be, except well into the forest land, I had no idea. Nor was I even sure in which direction the Keep lay. I could backtrail downstream and seek to return the way I had come. Only I had no doubt that were I to do so I would meet with Maughus and the hounds. Until those from the Keep had given up the hunt, I would not dare go back. Yet I must know whether it was Ursilla's creature that had taken the belt, leaving me more securely a prisoner than if I lay behind bolted and barred doors and stone walls.

Also, those in the woodlands who had friendship with the Clan people would certainly be alerted to give knowledge if they saw me. I knew that a pard was a beast seldom if ever found this far north—being more truly native to the southwest Waste. At this very moment there could be spying eyes upon me—

The thought of that drove me once more back to the

rocks and the crevice. I hated to skulk within as if fear ruled me. However, prudence is sometimes a weapon when others fail. Let me, now that I was fed, lie up for the day and set out by night. The great cats are mainly creatures of the dark, and perhaps, with shadows about me, the fact that I was not one of those known to hunt in the woods would not be so easy to perceive.

My thoughts continued to worry away at me, so I got little sleep that day. I watched two of the small forest deer splash across the stream. The pard part of me responded with a message of meat, while the man noted their graceful trot and wished them well.

The man still alive in me—

That was the thought, which haunted me with dark and lingering dread. If I remained caught within the beast, how long might that man live? For perhaps the appetites and the desires of the pard would grow stronger and stronger with time, until there was no Kethan to be remembered or to control, only the cat to be hunted and slain if his enemies could encompass that.

Ursilla would know—she would rescue me—*if* I could reach her. There might be a fearsome price to pay for the bargain. And—

The other thought arose then. Would it ever be well to pay such a price? Might it not be better to remain a pard than yield wholly to Ursilla and my mother, lose all command of my own destiny, held by their reins as if I were one of the plodding, heavy-footed horses that had no other life in this world than to haul the wains, their years lived out in the harness put upon them by uncaring men?

I could not utterly suppress the sense of excitement and freedom that was returning now that the chase was well behind me. To be a prisoner—no! My pard side denied that. Better death than to be caught in Ursilla's net. Still— if I could gain the belt—without any bargain?

To dream of that was foolish indeed. I knew I was no match for Ursilla—a trained Wise Woman. How could I dare to think that I might win in any contest between us?

A Wise Woman—

I raised my head from my paws, causing a twitch of pain in the talon slashes by my sudden movement.

There was more than one Wise Woman in Arvon. And there were others too—the Voices—the many who had mastery of one part of the Power or another. There were those right here in the forest who might not be well disposed toward all humankind, but who might be tricked or wheedled into sharing some part of their knowledge.

That was a wild thought, one that had little hope of ever becoming a plan I could put into action. Yet it began to fill my mind, and the excitement born of the belt fed its growing.

Of the Maid in the Forest and the Star Tower

By twilight I had slept a little and my hunger was once more awake. Though I ranged along the stream for some distance trying my fishing skill again, I had no luck. Either my first successes were due to some fleeting pity from Fortune, or else the fish had been warned by them, though the latter hardly seemed likely in such a short time.

Eat I must, and food that might have sustained me in my true form—berries, cresses and the like—would not suffice now. I must have meat, and the pard was fast taking command, induced by hunger into attempting a true hunt.

I was still padding along the riverbank when a rank smell alerted my animal senses. It was meat—on the hoof and not too distant. As they had during my escape from the Keep, the set of beast instincts claimed me. I was now all pard and not man.

Two bounds carried me to the top of a ridge of stone. A light breeze blew toward me, bearing a heavy reek from my destined prey. My eyes, better adjusted to this twilight than human ones would be, marked well what snorted, grunted, snuffled and rooted below. A family of wild pigs, a fearsomely tusked boar in command, was moving toward the stream.

Even the pard hesitated to challenge such a formidable opponent. The boars were noteworthy as one of the greatest perils of the forest, rightly feared by even those who would dare to tree a snow cat. Their tusks were wickedly sharp, and the creatures had a sly cunning that they used well when trailed. It was known that they sometimes doubled back to set an ambush for any hunter foolish enough to track them in their own territory.

Surprise would be my best weapon. I crept along the stone, flowing forward in that silence native to the feline species when they find need to employ it.

Though the younger pigs, even the sow, looked to be better eating, I knew that the boar must be my quarry, since with him disabled or dead, the greatest danger would be gone. My muscles tensed for the leap.

The sow, with her piglets and two half-grown older offspring, had snorted on a length ahead. The boar was tearing up the ground with his tusks as if he dug for some delicacy he had sniffed lying below the surface.

I sprang, giving voice to no cry. And I landed true, the weight of my body bearing the rank-smelling animal under me to the ground. My jaws made a single, sharp snap, and I delivered a blow with one paw, putting into it all the force I could summon. The boar lay still, his neck broken, dead in an instant.

Then I heard grunting and raised my head, voicing a warning snarl of my own. The sow now faced me, her litter sheltered behind her, rage plain to read in every line of her body.

I snarled again, watching the small, red eyes. Would she attack? While not having the strength of her mate, she was still such a fighter when cornered as to make any attacker think twice. I crouched lower over the body of the boar, readying for a charge if she showed fight.

The young pigs squealed, uttering a thin, ear-troubling sound, and the two older ones pawed the ground. Yet they made no move, seeming to wait for some unheard order from their dam.

When the sow did not rush, I decided she was only on guard for her young. I took hold of the body of my kill, retreated slowly backward, ever watching the sow. She continued to grunt, lowering her head to tear at the trampled soil with her lesser tusks. Though the picture of seething rage, she did not move toward me.

At last she raised her heavy head, gave a final grunt, and whirled with a speed I thought uncommon to her species. Driving her litter before her, flanked by the two older pigs, she had the whole family on the run. I was left to drag my kill to the top of the ridge and there satisfy my hunger, firmly closing my human mind to what I did, allowing the pard full control.

Before I had finished, I heard small rustlings and knew that at a safe distance around me the scavengers, drawn by the scent of my feast, were gathering. When I was gone they would move in to fight and squabble over what remained, until only well-picked bones would lie among the rocks.

I had eaten, now I would drink—but farther on. I had no wish to once more front the sow and her litter. Though I had faced her down once, if I came again and seemed to threaten her piglets, I could well have such a struggle as would mean grave danger. Again Fortune had favored me in that quick, sure kill from which I had come unmarked. There was no reason to exhaust my luck by too frequent testings of it.

The moon was rising slowly. Its reflection did not yet shimmer on the water as I drank deeply and then sat down to lick clean my fur. My hunger and thirst satisfied, my beast nature was lulled. I was ready to think again.

The plan for seeking out some forest Wise One to aid me seemed very thin and difficult to follow. Yet I dared not so soon return to the vicinity of the Keep where I was certain Maughus and his huntsmen waited. Or would my mother and Ursilla bring such pressure to bear that he would have to abandon his plan for ridding himself of the obstacle that I was? There was no way of guessing what passed behind me. It was better to turn all thoughts to what might lie about or before me at this moment.

As I lingered by the stream, my ears and eyes reported what action they could detect. I heard movement among the trees, picked up scents. Huge-winged night moths hovered over the water feeding on smaller winged things that rose from the reeds or stream edge. Now and then another airborne marauder swooped upon the moths to take a victim. About me the land, air, water seethed with life as I had never been aware of it when I had walked as a man.

Since I still had no other guide, I decided to travel along the stream. There were game trails that came down to the water here and there. Perhaps I might find one that also served men or beings enough like men to be approached. On so slender a hope I must hang for a time.

Though I picked up many scents as I prowled, never was there one that my pard self did not recognize as animal. If I did cross the territory of any of the forest people, such was not made known to me, even by my new, keener senses. At length, I began to despair of ever finding an intelligence of the sort to comprehend my troubles.

It was when my hope had reached the lowest point, was near vanishing indeed, that I heard low singing not born from the rippling water to my left. The notes, rising and falling in a cadence near that of a chant, drew me.

I lifted my head as high as I might, awaking twinges again from the claw wounds on my back, sniffing the night air. Human! There was before me someone of the species I had once been before the curse of the belt imprisoned me. And any human who chose the forest for a place of dwelling should surely be in touch with the Power!

Among the trees I stalked, the chant growing ever louder as I went. I could distinguish words now, but they had no mind-meaning. Still, that they were of the Power was made manifest by the tingling in my hide, the answering excitement they engendered. No man can pass unshaken when some sorcery is at work nearby.

At last I crouched behind a fallen tree, gazing out into a glade where the moon shone clearly upon a pillar of glistening, flashing quartz—gemlike with life-fire beneath its light. For life of a sort coiled and flowed within its length, moving with the constant play of some imprisoned flame.

At the column foot, encircling it, grew a mass of plants, each one crowned with a single silver-white flower, which mirrored in miniature the moon above, under which they opened their petals as if they thirsted for the same light. They gave forth a subtle perfume as fresh as any spring-time breeze, though this was the autumn season.

From behind the pillar of cold flame came the singer. She rested against one hip a wide, flat basket into which she dropped bloom heads she snapped from among the flowers. And as she made her choice she chanted.

In the moonlight her body was as white and fair as the harvest she was culling. Her only garment was a belt

about her slender waist, from which depended a short
fringe of skirt giving forth soft tinklings at her every move.
This fringe was fashioned of silvery disks strung on fine
chains, a number spaced on each chain.

Between her small, young breasts hung the symbol of
the horned moon, appearing carved of the same flaming
crystal as the pillar about which she paced. Her long, dark
hair was fastened at the nape of her neck with a band of
silver, but strands brushed behind her fringed skirt, so
long were the locks.

I had never seen her like, even among the forest folk.
My pard nose told me she was human as to scent, yet no
maid from the Clans would walk alone in the forest rapt
in a ceremony of Power, performing some rite in the
moonlight. She must be a Wise Woman. Yet, she was as
different from Ursilla as the first beams of dawn light are
from the dregs of a long and dusty day.

Three times more she wove her path around the pillar,
plucking the flower heads until her basket was heaped
high. Then she took it in both hands and, standing so she
half-faced me, she held her harvest high, her face turned
up to the moon as she chanted louder. She might be so
giving thanks for what she had garnered.

Haw she beauty? I did not know, I could not judge
her by the standards of the Keep. But there was that in
me which struggled for freedom from my furred curse. In
that moment when I looked upon her so, I was all
inwardly a man, and a man drawn by the fairest that lies
in women.

So great was her Power (her own Power and not that
of the Wise Ones) upon me, that, without thinking, I
arose and advanced into the moonlight, forgetting the
guise I wore and all else. She had lowered the basket, and
now she looked straight at me.

There was startlement in her face.

That brought me to myself, would have sent me cow-
ering once more into cover. She steadied her basket once

again against her hip. Now her right hand moved in one of the signs that the initiated use for protection, or recognition.

The line she drew so in the air was visible, glowing as brightly as any flame torch for an instant. She spoke aloud as if asking me some question. But her words were strange ones I could not understand.

That I did not reply as she expected appeared to concern her. Once more she drew the sign as if to assure herself that it had been right. Then, as the lines disappeared, she spoke again, this time using the tongue of the Clans and the open land.

"Who are you, night treader?"

I tried to say my name. Only what came from my beast's mouth was a strange, guttural cry.

Now she pointed two fingers at me and spoke other Wise Words, watching me intently as she did so.

Once more I tried to speak. This time, to my sudden fear, I found that I could not move even my mouth. She had laid some spell upon me. Nor did she watch me longer, seeming to think that I was well held against any interference in her concerns. Leaving the pillar she neared the edge of the glade. There she set down her basket for a moment, to take up a hooded cloak within which she concealed her form, so that from moon silver she became in a short moment a gray shadow.

With the basket once more in her hold, she slipped away among the trees. I could have wept like a man who had lost his hope, or howled like a beast from which his rightful prey has been reft. But the bonds she laid upon me were as imprisoning as if she had lifted the crystal pillar and enclosed my body in it.

As I struggled with all my will to break free, the bonds began to loosen. At length I could move, if slowly. My strength returned little by little. As soon as I could stagger, I drew myself to the point where I had seen her disappear and there I set my beast sense to nose out her path.

Though I wavered along at first, sometimes striking against the tree trunks, my tread became firmer. I had to keep a slow pace lest I lose the track I followed. Even with the keenness of my sense of smell I found elusive the traces left by the one I sought, as if she had attempted to hide her trail.

Then the scent that guided me was gone, hidden in a wealth of odors, some sweet, some acrid, some spicy, the like of which I had not known before. I had come to the edge of another clearing many times the size of the one in which my youthful Wise Woman had performed her sorcery. This was no common forest glade, but rather a carefully tended garden.

The beds of growing things (things differing from the Harvest I had helped to garner from the fields of the Keep) spread outward from the foot of a Tower. Under the moon I could see that it also was unlike the buildings of the Clan in which I had been reared.

The forest structure was not round nor square, the two most common forms of towers, but five-pointed, like a large representation of the floor-painted star I had seen in Ursilla's private chamber.

Between each of the points was set a slender pole, reaching as high as some narrow windows that were visible in the second and third stories. The rods or poles gleamed with a faint light that surrounded the Tower itself with a haze. I guessed they might be some form of protection perhaps far more effective than any known to the Clans. The stone of the Tower itself under its radiance had a glisten quite unlike the rough look of normal blocks, and was a dull blue-green.

There was also a glow of light in several of the windows that I could see as I crept about the outer rim of the clearing to view the Tower from all sides. That this was the home of my Moon Witch I did not doubt. Nor did I believe she lived there alone. As I approached the other side of the Tower from the place where I had first sighted it, I came upon a paddock with a stable shelter beyond. These were like the ones I had known and had none of the strange quality of the Tower. Several horses grazed in the paddock, two of them with colts by their sides.

They must have caught my scent as I moved, for their heads came up and the stallion trumpeted. As I did not approach any closer, he quieted and only trotted along the fence between me and his herd. That the rest of them did not show the frenzy my presence had always evoked in their species before surprised me. They returned to their grazing, and even the stallion stood quietly when I paused, his head turned so his eyes could watch my every move. Beyond his watchfulness, he displayed no fear.

I made the entire circuit of the clearing. The Tower had a single entrance to the north, a small door nigh indistinguishable from the wall, set in one of the crevices between the points. And about the whole of the building there was a feeling of secretiveness and—withdrawal was the only word that came into my mind—as if those who sheltered there had, by choice, little to do with the ways of men.

It was in my mind that they doubtless also possessed devices to ensure their privacy. Still, we who are of the Old Race know when anything is of the Shadow. And about the Star Tower there was no stench of evil to warn one away. I found a place under a bush beyond the garden where I could stretch my length and yet watch the door. In me hope was growing, if but feebly, once again.

Now and again I blinked at the dimly lighted window visible from my lair and wondered whether the Witch Maid was behind it. Why had she culled the moonflowers? What spells did she now raise with their aid? If I could only have answered her question!

I arose, circled a little, and lay down again. The night

was far along now. Already the moon had passed from
overhead. Now the dim light, behind the window above,
had been snuffed out. Only the haze from the poles
wreathed around the Star Tower.

My head sank forward to rest upon my paws. A small
breeze swept toward me, coming over the garden to load
itself with the odors of herbs. Now I knew this to be an
herb garden, larger than any I had ever seen, and with
the familiar were mixed many I could not put name to.
Paths marked with water-worn stones divided the ground
into beds for easier access to reach their crops.

Some plants there were already fading, falling early
into the dormant sleep of the cold season lying yet a
moon or so before us. Others waxed more vigorous as if
the dying of the growing year was an incentive for them
to produce more abundantly.

I knew only Ursilla's spell-weaving. In it, she made use
of herbs and spices—small amounts of the latter she
bought from traders. But the ones she grew were only a
handful compared to this abundance. And the Moon Maid
had been gathering flowers— Did she practice a Magic
that was centered on growing things—Green Magic?

Some men speak ignorantly of White Magic and Black,
meaning that which is wrought for the benefit of mankind
and that of the Great Shadow, which ever threatens him.
But those well into the Mysteries do not speak so—
rather they aver that Magic is divided otherwise, and
each part has both a dark and a light side.

There is Red Magic that deals with the health of the
body, physical strength, the art of war also. Secondly
comes Orange Magic, which is a matter of self-confidence
and strong desire. Yellow is the Magic of the mind,
needing logic and philosophy, that which the Thau-
maturgists most dealt in.

Green is the hue not only of Nature's growing things
and fertility, but also of beauty and the creating of
beauty through man's own efforts. Blue summons the

emotions, the worship of whatever gods men believe in, prophecy. Indigo is concerned with the weather, with storms and the foretelling by stars.

Purple is a force that is drawn upon warily, for it carries the seeds of lust, hate, fear, power—and it is far too easily misused. Violet is pure power among the spirits, and few, even of the Voices, can claim to harness it. While Brown is the Magic of the woods and glades, of the animal world.

Those of the woodlands about which I knew aught were learned in the Green and Brown. And of all Magics, these are the closest to the earth, the less easily misused.

However, no one with the talent ever draws upon one Magic alone, but mingles this spell with that, seeking to draw the innate energy of what is most inclined to the result the sorcerer desires. All can be misused, thus coming under the Shadow. But he or she who chooses that path reaches for a Power that may recoil eleven-fold upon them if they have a stronger desire than they have talent.

The Green Magic of the place soothed me as I breathed in the odor of the herbs, and with it the subtle rightness of the garden. If I could only make known to those who dwelt here the curse laid upon me, it could well be that they would have that which would aid me.

That night I carried hope with me into slumber, no longer caring that the predawn light was banishing the haze of the rods by the Tower and that the day world stirred toward wakefulness. To one thought did I hold as I slipped helplessly into what was near a drugged sleep— that here I might find—not friends, for that much I did not hope—but someone who would understand—and— just perhaps—offer me aid.

Of How I Dreamed
and of What Ill Followed

I was in a far place, a place wholly alien to those of my kind— My kind? What species dared I now claim kinship with? For I was very much aware in this place that two natures seethed within me. Also, they did not lie quietly together in partnership, but rather carried on a ceaseless struggle for domination, now one and then the other rising into short-termed control.

However, in this place, each of the natures, so at war, made temporary pact, for they were both threatened. How I was so sure of that I could not tell. And the double identity that was me, twined and uneasily united for the nonce, was moving—

I did not walk in the body in that place beyond my waking comprehension. No, it was more as if I were a floating leaf drawn along by wind, the force of which could not be withstood.

I did not see with the eyes of man or beast. Rather I perceived what was about me by another sense I could not put name to. Thus I knew that I moved through a world of grayness in which naught had true solidity, only shadows. Very uncanny were most of the shadows among which I whirled. Some, I thought, had the aspect of beasts, some were monsters. Others took the form of men and women. From them always came an aura of soul-shaking fear or horror, so that I shrank from any near contact with them.

None appeared to notice me, or even be aware of each other. Each was enwrapped in a private world of fear and despair. They were not drawn as I was, but fluttered unhappily here and there as if in search, a search for which there was no end.

The farther I went the more complete and substantial became the Shadow forms. From gray wisps of mist they darkened, grew more dense. Now they did not drift above the ground: they ran breathlessly with sudden darts and halts. A few crept far more slowly, as if their own dark bodies were heavy burdens they could not escape.

These I saw the clearer because there hung a spark of light ahead. That was what drew me, though the other dark forms about me seemed oblivious of it. I had no choice, no escape. In me fear now arose to war with horror, as if my two selves were aroused once more to do battle. That was not so, for both man and beast cowered before the threat the spark of light suggested.

Brighter the gleam grew. From it, rays spread to reveal more of this land beyond all normal lands. Here were knife-sharp ridges, deep valleys between, as cups filled with utter darkness that emitted subtle promises of peril beyond my understanding.

I did not climb the ridges. Thankfully, I did not descend into the valleys, as I saw some of the other Shadow people do, to be swallowed up and lost. The current of air bore me on and on. Things rooted on the stone writhed, tossed long tendrils into the air. Those the shadow figures strove to avoid, as one flees a poisonous growth.

The light had become so bright as to dazzle whatever sense I used for sight in this place. Then it began to pulse. I knew—then I knew—that the light was formed by words, that it was my summons through some spell laid upon me.

There was no escape. Bound by strong ensorcellment, I was drawn to the source. Before it, I hung helplessly, forced to face the glare. Thus I perceived that what I confronted was a window, an opening in the fabric of this world. Through that the spell forced me to look—

The glare was five-pointed, a huge star the lines of which were formed by orange fire. In the center of the blaze stood one whom I could not distinguish, so bright and searing was the light about the muffled figure.

But the sorcery she wrought reached out for me.

Ursilla!

So she willed me back into her control. She would—

Frantically, I fought. Man and beast forged themselves into one for resistance. I had no real defense to set against her witchery, nothing but my will. However, that will was strengthened by what lies within all living things, the refusal to accept extinction without a battle. Perhaps such defense was the stronger in me during that moment because of my dual nature. I only knew that if I answered the call Ursilla gave, that which was truly Kethan would cease to be. There would remain only the part of me she could render totally submissive to her command.

The star formed a furnace of fire, scorching me. Ursilla's anger at my stubbornness fed the fire. She would turn to other weapons, and those she had to hand, ready. Though she did not speak, her purpose was made clear to me. If I obeyed now—then a portion of Kethan would survive. If I caused her to exert the force necessary to chain me fully to her purpose, then the inner core of me would become one of the shadowy seekers running hopelessly across this alien land. What might return to my own time and place would be a husk she could fill with another entity utterly obedient to her.

The orange fire of dominance and rule was changing, deepening into another more forbidding hue. Ripples of the other color flooded out from the points. There was very little left now—the purple of dire danger spread. Return to her—or be destroyed!

Yet the united spirit in me, fearful, terrified as it was, could not surrender. I knew the penalty, but there was part of the identity of Kethan that could not obey, that could not allow Ursilla to have her way. I did not know from whence that utter abhorrence of her offered bargain came, only that it held me firm.

Then—

There was a great tearing across the star, now almost entirely ominous purple. The points burst apart, even as the Shadow country was pulled away, as if a fabric were being rent with calm intent. Into one of the gaps of utter darkness that appeared within the rents, I swayed, dropped, unable to control my going.

The sensation of heat continued, though it was no longer as severe as the burning tongues that had whipped from the star point to sear me. I opened my eyes into the light of midday, where the sun hung like a ball of fire overhead.

My transition had been too abrupt. I was still dazedly lost between the Shadow world and the real. But, as my senses returned, I saw the woman who stood on one of the paths radiating out from the points of the Star Tower, those that divided the herb garden into sections.

Memory returned slowly. I raised my head, knew that I was still a pard, caught in the beast trap. Something had saved me from Ursilla, for the moment—that I understood. I gazed wonderingly up at the woman, sure that my escape was her doing.

She was not my Moon Girl, though she was as slender of body. And her face was youthful, save for her eyes, which carried years of full wisdom mirrored in them. Though she was plainly a woman, yet she wore breeches, a jerkin, both of green to blend with the plants knee-high around her.

Her hair was tightly plaited, the braids wound about her head to form a soft crown of dark brown in which there was a tinge of ruddy light. Also, her skin was an even brown, as if her life was spent much in the open.

Beside her feet was a basket in which lay bunches of newly gathered herbs. But my gaze centered on what she held between her two hands, its tip pointed straight at me. Just so might a man hold a spear, to warn off an enemy, or in defense.

I recognized a wand of Power, yet this was unlike the rune-engraved one that Ursilla kept in her most private box, for it was not carved of bone with mystic words inlaid in black and red. Instead, the woman's rod more resembled a freshly peeled branch, straight, unknotted. At the tip, turned toward me, was a single outstretched leaf, shaped like a spearpoint, of a very bright green.

As I stared at the woman, just as straightly did she regard me, her eyes as searching as Ursilla's could ever be. This, too, was a Wise Woman, though I sensed that the Powers she served were not the same as the ones to which Ursilla gave homage when she called.

"Who are you?" The woman did not lower her wand-spear. I believed that were I to make some hostile move, I would speedily discover it far more than a peeled branch with only a leaf at its tip.

I could shape no words. When I tried, there was only that sound akin to a strangled grunting.

She held her head a fraction to one side as if she listened.

"Sorcery," she spoke again. "Strong of the Power, but not well done. In the night I felt you come. Now—you draw that which is not of our world. That we cannot allow. To let even a hint of Darkness brush close to us—No!" She shook her head vigorously.

I gave my beastly cry for help. If this Wise Woman had destroyed Ursilla's attempt to reach me (for I was certain she had been the one to rend apart the Shadow world), then perhaps she could save me—point a way to my escape from this body.

Slowly, I drew myself forward. Out of the bush where I had sheltered, I crept belly down. Perhaps with my body I could display my need, ask voicelessly for her aid. Thus I abased myself as best I could.

The leaf point was no longer held unflinchingly aimed at my head. In her hands the wand swung a little, back and forth. Bright as the day was, its tip wrote on the air symbols in trails of green smoke that quickly dissipated.

"No," she denied me. "When the Dark strikes and evil walks the land, then we do not open our gates to any sorcery that carries the stench of the Shadow about it. I know not who you are, nor why you have brought your trouble hither. And there is naught that I can do for you. To let you remain— Even," she hesitated, "even if you could. I do not believe that one such as you can enter into our safety. If you can—then that might be another matter—"

Her first firm denial appeared to weaken a little. I crept on. But, as I would set paw upon the edge of that same path in which she stood, there was a flash of green. The glimmer did not spring from her wand, but from the ground before me, while the paw that I had so reached out tingled with pain. I had stubbed it against some unseen wall of protection. What she had said was plainily the truth, her circle of Green Magic rejected me.

The shock of the rejection loosed the control of my man nature. For a moment I was no longer Kethan encased in a beast body that was a prison. Rather, I was a pard aroused to the full anger such a creature felt when its fierce desire was thwarted. My tail lashed, I raised my voice in a roar of animal rage. I sprang, only to be defeated by that invisible defense.

Now the woman's expression changed. She raised her wand in one hand and brought it down in a lashing blow on the air. But across the painful scratches the bird had inflicted on my back there was a sudden hot agony, although her wand had been far from physically touching my body.

I screamed a cat's full-throated scream, the pain feeding my anger, pressing the man back into close confinement in my mind. Kill—Kill! Almost I could hear the words as if such a command had been shouted in the ears now folded back against my skull. Again I snarled and struck out at the barrier that kept me from what was now surely my prey.

Once again her wand lashed the air. The blow fell truly across my wounded back and flanks. Dimly, even the beast could recognize that I was helpless, that to continue our unequal struggle would mean only more pain for me. With a last snarl, I slunk in retreat to the woods. Nor did I look back.

As I went, the man once more fought his way to freedom. The pard was under my control. My sense of failure was as grievous to my mind as the strokes had been across my body. My aborted attack had certainly closed all ways of communication with those in the Star Tower. And I was as certain, as if the woman herself had sworn it by some Name of the Power, that only there I might have found a measure of aid.

Now I did not care where I went. There was no lasting

hope I might locate some other inhabitant of the forest who would be willing to play my friend. There were others who might offer me shelter—for their own purposes. But those I must avoid with as much energy as I would Ursilla.

The woman of the Tower had delivered me from Ursilla's attack. However, she had done that only because the stir of such sorcery had in some way threatened her own safety. That I could count on such a gift of Fortune again, I greatly doubted. Ursilla might not weave the same spell, but she had others as powerful, perhaps many of them.

My unplanned wandering had brought me back, I saw, to the small glade where the pillar and the moonflowers stood. In the sunlight, the latter were tightly closed, showing only gray-green buds and a few badly withered, dead flower heads, while the pillar itself lacked the core of fire that had blazed high during the night. I hesitated under the branches of one of the trees that made up the walling of the enchanted place. Was this also closed to me? I had the haunting belief that some Power that was benign might shield me from Ursilla's seeking. Where I could find such—?

I sank to the crouch the pard used preparing for a leap upon a quarry. Then, as I had done when I uselessly abased myself before the Wise Woman of the Tower, I crept forward inch by inch.

This time there was no heady perfume from the tightly closed flowers, no sense of enchantment and beauty. It would seem that the sorcery had departed, for I was able to enter into the moon garden, even reach the pillar, feeling no discharge of energy as I had the night before.

I touched nose to the pillar. It was stone, not crystal—dead stone. Nothing lingered here any longer to feed my hope.

Slowly, I retreated. The river again—for I was hungry. However, my hunger was only partly of the flesh. All my life, though I had lived close among my fellows, I had been as one set apart. That loneliness I had only half known for what it was, but in this hour the full desolation of it settled upon me, as a yoke of sword steel set about my throat, chaining me to that which was myself, which could never be one in thought or life with any other.

There were the Wereriders—

Dully, I considered whether I might search them out, hope to claim a measure of acceptance from those who also were two shapes throughout their lives. But they were shape-changers by inheritance and choice, bred to that strangeness. Whereas with me it was truly, as my mother had warned me, a curse to separate me from the normal world.

Was this of the Lady Eldris's planning, so that I should be removed from Maughus's path by this estrangement? I could accept that. Just as I accepted Thaney's cry of "Kill!" when she had looked upon me over her brother's shoulder and his sword was bared ready to slay. I had no tie with my betrothed to regret.

My mind picture of Thaney as I last saw her faded. There was another now, so sharply etched in my mind that I might be viewing her again just as I had watched her in the moonlight, all crystal and life, holding her basket of flowers on high. Witch Girl—Moon Singer— Yet she was of the Star Tower, firm closed against me.

The river flowed below. I went down upon an out-thrust bar of sand that near divided the stream at that point, dropping my muzzle into the water's coolness, drinking deep. Perhaps it was the assuaging of a thirst, I had not realized I had, that banished all fancies to the back of my mind, alerted me to the necessity of living by the hour that was present, not in the past, or anticipating what might be a darksome future.

Once more I fished and found that Fortune favored me with two scaled bodies that I devoured eagerly, leaving not even an edge of spiky fin for any scavenger. The life about me was that of the normal forest world. I sensed no enemy, neither hunter, nor of the Power.

Jutting from the earth at an angle, I found a rock that was shelter from the heat of the sun. Beneath that I lay down, though I feared to sleep, lest I return into the dream Ursilla had spun for my entrapment. If Kethan so feared, the pard's body was oblivious to such dangers. It is natural for any cat, large or small, to sleep more hours than a man. And I could not escape the needs of my present shape.

I roused again near twilight. Probably the beast instincts acted as a goad to drive me out of a slumber, mercifully this time untroubled by dreams. But, as I raised my head and gazed about, I was aware of danger.

What the danger was, or from whence it came, I could not determine. I only knew that my heart beat faster, my lips wrinkled back in a noiseless snarl that was the reaction of the pard. It was only after a moment or two of seeking to identify by my natural sense what threatened me now that I knew the peril was not of the natural world, but stemmed from another plane of existence. Ursilla! The conclusion that she had traced me, was about to resume the struggle between us, followed the recognition instantly.

My unplanned reaction was flight. I was out of my half cave, on the move with the wide bounds of a feline, before I had more than realized what might be the matter. In the open, came speedily the knowledge that I was not the only quarry who chose to run.

Paying no attention to me, who by nature was their enemy, two of the small forest deer matched my speed, drew away, their eyes showing the whites of fear. Before them, at a hard run, pounded three of the wolves who are so rarely seen by men of the Clans that they are near legend. Smaller things rustled in the shrubs and tall grass that bordered the river at this point, showing furred rumps now and then as they fled.

I was startled when I understood that I alone was not the hunted, and my conviction that this was some play of Ursilla's was shaken. However, the terror that kept me in flight mounted when I tried to pause, until fear was commander in my mind, sending me headlong in a senseless race with all the rest.

There were sometimes hunts, out in the open, where men gathered with beaters to scare up the animals, drive them witless with fright toward waiting marksmen. To my Kethan mind, this present assault upon my nerves bore a distinct relation to that. Yet there came no sound of horn, no brazen clamor behind me. Nor would such have sent me headlong in this fashion.

We *were* being hunted. Only the hound that coursed us was a thing out of the Dark, the mere emanation of which was enough to start this stampede. When I settled upon that explanation it seemed to me a certain measure of my panic departed and I was able to regain a little control over my reactions to what drove us.

I began, not to slacken speed, for that I soon discovered I was not able to do, but rather to edge toward the right as I went. For I noted an oddity about this fleeing company, they ran along a single path across country—as if they must keep to a foreordained road.

More and more I angled right, until I had reached what I thought was the very edge of the fugitives' way. There I gathered all my strength for one great leap—not ahead—but to the side—

My pard body arched through the air. Then—

I could not command my muscles. Falling, my full panic was reborn, to fill my whole mind, drive out intelligence, leave only the beast's fear. In a second, I would dash against the earth.

But—

Something closed about me. I lunged, twisted, to find myself tight prisoner, wound about by sticky cords. I was netted!

Of the Snow Cat and What Chanced in the Haunted Ruin

My struggles were to no avail. Such writhing only drew about me more tightly the cords of the trap into which I had fallen. And, where the bonds crossed my hurts, they stung like living fire until I screamed aloud my pard's squall of pain and terror.

What held me so was part of a web. Fighting to think clearly, to overcome my witless fear by human senses, I could perceive a resemblance, in the now torn strings wrapping me around, to the small webs one finds in the early morning spread in lacy patterns, pearled with dew, in garden and field.

What kind of creature could weave this—a web large enough to hold securely a plunging, fighting pard? That was a chill thought as my struggles grew less, my Kethan mind gaining control.

No man of my own people had ever ventured far into the forest or the hills beyond. Our knowledge of the forbidden country was limited to a handful of second-hand impressions and stories. There were strange creatures aplenty to be seen or met therein, that most men were united in believing. And few of them were ready to welcome my kind—save as prey.

My fighting against the web had tethered me to a tall standing rock. This, I now saw in the light of day, bore deeply incised carvings, which were so old and timeworn that it was difficult to distinguish any real pattern from their curves and lines.

A second such pillar reared some feet away, and it was between the two that the web had been anchored. My struggles had ripped the lines into streamers that had caught about me and the pillar against which I now half hung. Very thin and fragile the threads looked, but I could testify as to their strength.

As I tried to keep control, ceasing my plunging, examining them as best I could, I sensed something else.

Just as I had known that the Star Tower held no evil within its protective barriers, in fact, could be a refuge of sort against the Shadow, here was that reversed. From the pillar beside me came an emanation of cold, of a deadly chill to turn a man's heart and mind into frozen ice. The evil in the chill encased me in a loathsome effluence, as if I now sank slowly into the slime of a pestilent bog.

At first the evil was disembodied, a cloud without form or person. But the more it lapped around me, the more aware I became that it was in some way almost tangible.

And that I would face that —*thing*—and soon.

Shudders I could not control shook my body now. In spite of my furred skin I was naked to the freezing force of whatever Dark Thing had so entrapped me. There was nothing I might do, save wait helplessly for it to come—to—

Movement!

I tried to screw my head farther around, to see more plainly what I had only glimpsed from the corner of one eye. This was an effort, but I managed to achieve a twisted angle of my head that gave me a wide range of vision.

The two pillars between which I was prisoner were backed by a tumble of rocks. No—not *rocks!* They were, in spite of the erosion of time, too carefully shaped. There had once been a building there—the pillars mounting guard before it.

Now the ancient blocks had fallen in upon each other in a heap. No grass had rooted about them, though the cracks were filled with a bleached looking earth. In fact, there was no vegetation within a wide area about the ruin. And in the middle of the rock pile gaped a dark hole.

There was a flicker of movement again within that. At last I had traced the evil to its source. The weaver of this web rested therein, viewing me with an avid pleasure that struck at my reason. I was prey!

Out of the hole, moved by stiff jerks, came a segmented leg. Upheld at the end of that a claw stretched wide enough to perhaps tear the throat out of my pard body. And, through the leg was covered by a hard encasing substance not unlike that of an insect carapace, yet at each joint of the segments there sprouted a tuft of course gray-white hair.

The claw closed upon one of the cords of the web that was still anchored to the pillar, applied a vigorous shaking that I tried to resist. That must have informed the lurking hunter that its trap did indeed enclose some living thing.

Leg and claw instantly snapped back into the hole. But that I had won no more than a very short respite I well knew. My neck ached at the stiff position of my head. Still I must face whatever might come at me from the lair.

The hole, the longer I stared into it, was not entirely black. There were small yellow points of light, very dim —but still there. I counted eight set in two rows. *Eyes!* Eyes surveying me, making sure I was safely a prisoner.

Beyond, the sound of the fleeing animals had died away. It seemed to me that I hung in a moment of utter silence—waiting— Then out of the hole came once more the leg—or arm—and then a second such! Beyond those only the eyes were visible, the rest of the creature lying deeper within the den.

I thought that I had screamed. Then I knew that the furious challenge had not burst from my throat, but another's. A furred shape flowed fluidly into my very limited range of vision, leaped, not at the hole into which the arms had whipped back at the sound, but to the top of the jumble of blocks that formed my enemy's den.

A snow cat! And a larger one than I had ever seen. The creature was in a snarling rage, its yellow eyes afire, its tail whipping from side to side. The gaze of the eyes fixed upon me and now it growled.

Well did I know the reputation of the giant hill cats. They were highly protective of their hunting territories, fighting to the death often to resist any invasion of the stretches of hill and forest that they considered their own. Save during the mating season, they held no contact with their fellows, walking alone and arrogant in their jealous pride.

That a pard was invading the snow cat's territory was indeed a challenge. However, I was already helplessly the prey of the lurker in the hole, no threat to this newcomer. Why did he then wish to attack?

The cat was a male, at the height of his strength and

might, I believed. Under other circumstances, I would have thought him a magnificent sight. But—perhaps death under his swift attack would be easier than that which the lurker had planned for me. Only no one welcomes death gladly.

Then—

I squalled again. Not from the pain of any wound, but from fear that struck me more severely than any rippling of claws. There was a *voice* in my mind!

That the Wise Ones could communicate so among their kind was well known. But they did it only when well trained and provided with certain safeguard barriers, so that such an invasion could be controlled and tempered. No ordinary human possessed such a talent, nor would welcome even the thought of it.

"Do not move!"

Did the lurker so warn me? Or the snow cat? Were the great felines thus able to communicate with their kind, unknown to men?

"Do not move." Again that command was impressed upon my mind.

The cat! Certainly it was the cat!

He was now pressed belly flat on the stone, inching forward to another block, a little lower, that rested directly above the hole. As he extended a paw to place on it, I saw the stone move a fraction. Quickly, the snow cat drew back. He bent his head, sniffed along the inner edge of the block. Or was he examining closely the way it rested upon its fellows?

Whatever he had discovered, made him crouch down and back. I could see muscles ripple under his hide, the telltale twitch of the dark tip of his silver-white tail. He did not advance now with exploratory stealth, rather he leaped, landing full force upon the suspect block.

It gave under him, crashing down. But so quick was the cat that he was again arching his body into the air in my direction even while the block he had loosened by the weight of his body smashed to earth, sealing the hole, perhaps for good.

One of his forepaws, as he landed, had caught in the sticky cords of the web. He did not fight as I had done so disastrously. Rather he moved with infinite caution, drawing back his paw so the broken portion of web was stretched out. Then, lowering it to earth, he sawed the thread back and forth across a drift of grit that formed the soil around the ruin.

Where my most frenzied struggles had produced nothing but a tighter prison, his delicate handling of his bonds broke the cord, loosed him. I would have followed his action if I could, but I was too tightly caught.

"Be still!" He varied his command, padding back and forth just beyond the tangle of the broken web, studying me and my bonds. Then he turned, was gone like a flash of silver.

I was left to my entrapment. The snow cat had bettered my fate by so much—the hole was sealed and no claws now reached for me. The quick death that had been before me could well now become a slow one of thirst and starvation, or of horror, if scavengers chanced upon me so helpless. I had to face that prospect bleakly.

My forepaws were thickly entangled. The pain where the web strands had fallen upon my scratched back and flanks was gone, but my hindquarters were numbed. I had—

Back into view moved the snow cat. He mouthed the end of a branch splintered and gnawed as if he had freed it from the parent tree by the action of his fangs. The leaves, crushed by being dragged along the ground, gave off a strong, nose-wrinkling odor, acrid enough to make me cough and my eyes tear as the cat approached.

He laid his burden down with care that none of the mangled leaves touch his own hide. Approaching, he eyed me and the tangled cord with an absorbed examination.

"Danger—" His thought reached me strongly. "Only way—do not move!"

Once more he grasped the branch in his jaws. Making a visible effort, he swung it clear of the ground, brought it around by the strain of his neck muscles, and dropped the length so that it lay with sap-oozing leaves directly across the strands of the web, but not touching me. There followed a puff that looked like steam rising from the cord.

Where the leaves touched the remnants of the web, it withered, blackened, gave off a nasty stench. Now the withering ran out from the actual contact, along the portions in which I was enwrapped. I felt as if my bonds were being burned away. Perhaps that was what was happening, for they fell from my body in tattered, blackened strands.

That I was free, was all that mattered. I lunged away from the pillar. Only I found it hard to move. The numbness in my hindquarters did not lessen. I staggered, would have fallen had the snow cat not moved up so that his shoulder touched mine, his strength kept me on my feet.

That he was no true cat, I had already begun to believe. Yet there was about him, as we moved slowly away from that pocket of evil, no taint such as had hung about the dweller in the ruin and its trap-web. Another Were? Dared I believe that I had found such?

As my companion shouldered and urged me back into the ground across which the wild hunt had pounded, I no longer sensed the compulsion to flee. That the lurker in the ruins had been the primary cause of that panic, driving the forest creatures, I did not believe. I was certain that what had sent such force to snap at one's heels was a harrowing hound of the Shadow.

The snow cat guided and supported me back toward the river. Slowly my hindquarters began to lose their numbness, but that was no favor from Fortune, for the wounds on my back began again to trouble me. The mounting pain of each step became a kind of red torment in my mind, and, at last, I moved in a haze of agony hardly aware of aught that lay around me.

Why I did not drop to the ground in my suffering I did not know. Save that just as I had been driven by some Shadow will earlier, so now I was kept moving by the determination of the snow cat. He did not again speak to me, mind to mind. However, there was a force radiating from him that acted as a goad of sorts.

In sight of the river he halted, his head up to sniff the air. About us were rocks and crevices. Toward one of those he nudged me. I crawled within, so spent that I thought each effort of raising a paw and putting it down once again was the last I could so endure.

There I crouched, my mouth dry, longing for the water of the stream I could hear from my hiding place, yet could not reach. The snow cat stood between me and the outer world, his stance one of he who waits. Through the ground under me I could feel, even as my pain-dulled ears could hear, the thud of trotting hooves. Men—? Hunters from the Keep?

If they saw the snow cat they would be after two trophies instead of one! He must be warned— Only I had not his trick of mind-speech, I could but utter a low growl.

"Not those you fear." He did not turn his head to look at me, but his message was clear. "Be silent—"

I could see the rider now. There was only one within sight. He rode clad in mail, an ornate battle helm on his head. Mounted on that was what appeared to be a life-size eagle, its wings half upraised as if prepared for flight. The horse he bestrode was not akin to those of the Clan fold, but plainly of the same blood as the ones I had seen pastured by the Star Tower, the hide dappled, the legs longer than normal.

As the rider noted the snow cat, he did not reach for the sword sheathed at his hip. Rather, he raised his gauntleted hand in salute as a man gives greeting to another he knows. Then the cat moved forward, leaping to a rock that brought his fanged head near on a level with the rider's.

Mount reined in, the rider, whose face was too much in the shadow of the helm for me to see clearly, sat easily in the saddle, facing the cat. Though I heard nothing, either with my ears, or my mind, I was certain that they spoke together by some method of their own.

I could see no belt about the body of the cat. If he were of the Werekin, then he needed no such key to change shape. Was he one of the Wereriders? Their territory was supposed to lie to the southeast of the Clan lands, but that would not prevent them from traveling elsewhere.

At length, the rider once more raised his hand to salute the cat. When he moved on, he changed directions, heading back the same way from which he had come. Had he brought some message?

The cat did not watch him go, but returned swiftly to where I lay. As he neared, his mind-speech was imperative.

"We must hurry. The Shadow is on the move!"

The part-buried man in me responded to the urge. I managed to waver to my feet. But my pard body was near spent. Somehow I staggered down to the water, felt that rise about my limbs, pasting my fur tight to skin. Again, his strength alone, pushing against me, brought me through the weak current, out onto the far bank.

There I sank down, utterly exhausted, though he nosed at me, trying to get me on my legs. Once more, I could hear a thud of hooves against the ground. The cat left my side, trotting purposefully toward the edge of the forest. Was the eagle-helmed rider returning, or was this indeed a hunter approaching, and my companion, having done his best for me, was prudently withdrawing?

At that moment neither guess mattered. I was far too

spent to care. Apathetically I watched, unable to raise my head any to widen my field of vision. The cat had halted by the first tree, once more waiting.

From under the shade of branch and leaves moved a rider leading another horse by the reins. I knew her— the Moon Witch; though this time her white body was clothed in breeches, boots, shirt and jerkin of green and brown intermingled so that only when she had advanced fully into the open, could I see her clearly.

The cat reared up, setting his paws against her saddle blanket on either side of her leg, the mount showing no alarm at the beast's move but standing quietly. She leaned over a little so that they stared eye to eye, then she nodded.

From the breast of her jerkin she pulled some small object, which hung there on a chain. With this in her hand, as if it might be a weapon, she came purposely toward me, the cat trailing behind.

Before she reached my side, the girl slid from her light saddle, her mount standing quietly with the reins dropping to the ground. She came to me, swinging in her hand from its chain a round globe of crystal. Within it was imprisoned a sprig of some sort of vegetation, green and glowing.

The Moon Witch swung the chain to encircle my head as I raised it at her coming. Then the ball with its sprig of green came to rest just below my throat. I—

I was a man!

My fur was gone, my skin was visible, though I had not regained my belt. I was—back!

The shock of the transition without warning was so great, my world swung dizzily to and fro. I was aware of her hands on me, that I was being lifted, carried. I was laid across a saddle and caught my breath at the pain of the jolting, which each step of the horse caused me.

Someone mounted up, raised me, though his touch on my back nearly tore a scream from my dry throat. For this was a man, not my Moon Maid who tended me, though from whence he had suddenly appeared, I had no knowledge.

I had a blurred impression of a dark head bent over me, a thin face, well browned by sun and weather, above which the hair peaked sharply. His was a secret face, one to keep thoughts and words locked well within. Like the Tower woman, one might have judged the stranger in the flowering of youth, but the eyes, yellow as any cat's, were old—weary and old.

The eyes held mine. No mind-speech came to me, only a kind of force. It drove me steadily away from consciousness into a darkness where pain was gone and time no longer mattered.

Yet I was not entirely overborne by the stranger's will. As if I sensed from a very far distance, I knew we rode on and the forest held us again. I was convinced, as well, that the stranger who held me meant me no harm, rather good. Also that I must not trouble myself with such matters now—but withdraw, to regain my strength and will. The wonder of my change held—the Moon Maid's magic had wrought this. On my breast, I felt warmth spreading from the pendant she had put on me. That talisman I must hold to so I remain a man.

Of Those in the Tower and How I Chose Danger

I lay face down, my head turned to one side so that before my bemused eyes I saw only stone blocks of a wall. Across my back rested something cooling, soothing, drawing from my wounds the pain of the fire that had lain within the ragged furrows since I had won from the web trap. I heard voices behind me, not in my mind this time.

"The moly will lose its power soon. What then, my Lord?"

It was a woman who spoke so. A challenge hung in her tone.

"We must discover who he is, from whence he comes. I do not believe from the Gray Towers. Yet what other Werestrain walks this land? And he is not of the Shadow. If he rouses before the change, perhaps this we can learn—"

A man—he whom I remembered holding me before him as we rode from the river? But where did I lie? And who were they who had tended me? My passage from sleep to waking became complete as I felt that I must know answers to those questions.

I levered myself up a little on the bed and turned my head, to face those who stood beyond.

Yes, that was the man who had come to my rescue. The Moon Witch did not accompany him as I had hoped. Rather, there stood the woman of the herb garden who had driven me into exile. Why had she now given me both shelter and tending? I must be within the Star Tower, for I could see that the walls behind the two who were regarding me were oddly angled. The chamber must be shaped to fit into one of the points of the star.

"Who are you who have given me shelter?" I asked when neither of them spoke.

The woman came to my side. Her cool fingertips rested for a moment on my forehead. There was a faint perfume of spicy growing things coming from her hand, as if she had but lately been at labor in her garden.

"His fever is gone," she said. Now she stripped the covering from my back, so I felt the small chill of air striking my shoulders and hips. Again, she touched here and there along what must have been the wounds the hawk had set upon me. "Healing well, the poison being stayed," was her second verdict.

"You ask who we are." She moved around into my full sight. "We are those who dwell apart, asking naught of any man save that we be left to follow our own ways."

There was no welcome in her face, nor was there outright rejection either. She might be waiting for me to take some action, speak some word, on which she could base her judgment of whether I was friend or foe. Yet, for all her reserve of emotion, I knew I could never name her enemy. There was that about her which argued that she abhorred the Shadow in all its ways.

"And who are you?" It was the man who came a stride forward to stand beside her.

"I am—was—Kethan—heir to Car Do Prawn of the Redmantle Keep. What I am now—I do not know."

I was sure I had seen a fleeting change of expression on his face when I named myself. Had Maughus's hunters spread so far the news of my escape that it had reached this quiet place? Still I could not accept that this man or woman would yield to any pressure from such as Maughus. For they had about them both, like a cloak about the body in the months of cold, an elusive suggestion of Power. I could feel of them partly as I did toward Ursilla, that they saw and did things beyond the talent of mankind.

"Car Do Prawn," repeated the man. "Lord Erach rules there, but if you are heir—" He gazed at me interrogatively.

"I am son to the Lady Heroise, his sister."

"That is a clear human line," the man continued. "How came you then under the Were spell? Was it laid upon you?"

"By my folly, as Ursilla and my mother said, because of the belt—"

"Let him tell his story later." The woman interrupted me. "I think it is time for the cordial. He must be strengthened or the moly will fail the sooner."

I did not understand her meaning. However, when the man aided me to sit up and she brought me a cup of steaming liquid, I obediently emptied that even though the taste was bitter. As I so drank, another came into the chamber.

My Moon Witch! Again she wore the riding garb

wherein I had seen her by the river. Behind her trailed two tawny shapes that I knew for wild cats half-grown. That any could tame them was a mystery, for such beasts are noted for their fierce natures. Yet, they rubbed about her ankles lovingly, hindered her so in walking that she must pick up the bolder, holding it within the crook of her arm, fondling its ears.

"There is a pied hawk in the air," she said. "It has four times circled the garden. I do not think it hunts—but rather watches."

"So—" The woman nodded, then looked to me.

"The wounds you bear, Clansman. They were scored by a hawk's talons. What enemy have you?"

"One only with the Power—the Wise Woman, Ursilla," I mumbled. The girl had been so intent upon her message that she had not looked to me. Now she turned full gaze in my direction. Within me another magic worked, one that bore no kinship with the Power.

I had seen her first in the majesty of one who speaks with what is greater than any of our species, robed herself with the Power. And then again I had seen her through feverish eyes by the river. Three times—still within me it was as if I had known her all my life. Or else had been aware there was such a one in the world and had unconsciously sought her. Yet she looked upon me with indifference. The cub she fondled might be of far greater importance to her.

"The Wise Woman Ursilla— She dwells at Car Do Prawn?" the man asked.

"Since my mother returned from Garth Howel. I do not—" I hesitated. To reveal myself so much less a master of my own destiny in the eyes of the Moon Maid, that was a hard thing. Yet there could only be truth with these three—that I knew.

"Ursilla is not fully my enemy. She would have me do her will. Therefore—her creature (I am sure it was *her* hawk) took the belt. Now she perhaps seeks me again."

"Tell me more of this belt," the man ordered with some of the same authority in his voice as Pergvin used when instructing me in arms.

So I told my tale, of the gift of the belt, the transformation that it wrought in me, of how Maughus had used that to force my flight from the Keep, and the later attack of the hawk.

"Thus without the belt, you believe that you cannot return to man form?" the man asked when I had done.

"I thought not—until now. But—what did you do for me, Lady," I dared to ask the girl directly, "that made me a man once more?"

She pointed and I looked down to where there swung against my bare breast the small ball of crystal, within it the sprig of green, which to my eyes now did not seem so perfect, having a slightly withered appearance.

"Moly," the Moon Witch replied. "The herb that can counteract any spell, until it dies. But when it dies," she shrugged, "you will return to the pard, unless you learn better what can be done."

It seemed to me that there was a kind of contempt in her gaze, as if I showed such stupidity in my past actions that I was hardly worth any tending. My feeling for her recoiled a little, to be tinged in turn with anger. Who was she to judge me so?

The man paid no attention to her, rather he gave me an order.

"Put forth your hand!"

When I had done so, he cupped his under mine, raising my palm closer to study the lines that met and crossed there. I saw again his faint change of expression.

"It is not the belt that wrought your change." His words were blunt. "That only provided a key to open the door. Unfortunately, because it was the key, your guess that this Wise Woman can use it to control you now is the truth. And also—if the belt is destroyed—"

"I will be only pard?" I demanded when he hesitated.

"As it now stands, yes," he admitted.

"And if Maughus gains the belt—then that is what he will do—destroy it!" The strength that had come back into my body made me want to leap from the bed, return forthwith to the Keep. If I fronted Maughus as a man I could challenge him and— But what had the maid said concerning this moly? I peered intently into the globe. There was no mistaking that the sprig within was dying.

"Can I get another?" I held up the globe to demand of the three.

The woman shook her head. "Only once can the spell work for the same person."

"Meanwhile—" The girl still stroked the cub she held. The other had reared up to paw at her breeches. "The hawk flies overhead. Maybe so some other shall learn who shelters here—"

"Not so—yet." The woman contradicted her. "I have set the spell—"

"It is not working," the girl returned flatly. With that report, she startled both her companions.

The woman hurried from the room, the girl after her. I looked to the man for an explanation, to find that he was studying me.

"A spell-tie then," he said slowly.

"What mean you?"

"Just this—you are tied to the belt. And the belt lies beyond these walls, in the hands of one with Power."

"So—as long as I am here," I caught his meaning, "I am a breech in your defenses—?"

"For now it does not matter." He shrugged as if it really did not. "Tell me more of this wandering trader of yours, this Ibycus. What manner of man was he?"

"My mother said he was more than he seemed. She believed he confided in the Lady Eldris the secret of the belt so she could use it against me. I—I also thought he wore trading for a cloak."

"If this be so—why then did you accept the belt?"

"Because—once I looked upon it I desired it so greatly I could not help myself." I told him the truth, even though it might well name me a weakling, easily defeated by my own desires. I did not know why I wished so to stand well in the regard of this stranger. From the first, he had had to save me from the results of my own folly.

That all three of the dwellers within the Star Tower regarded me as a lesser being, whose concerns made them impatient, I guessed. The assessment made me wish for some way in which I could prove to them that I was not the nothing of their accounting.

"The belt—" I put now into words what I had felt. "It made me—free—"

"Still, now it has bound you," he pointed out. "And for such binding there is only one remedy."

"That being?" To get the belt back from Ursilla? To win my own form again and destroy it? I pelted him with questions.

"The belt is the key, you must learn to use it."

"How?" I demanded.

"The answer lies within yourself, and only you can seek it." His answer was ambiguous. "But of this I am sure. Car Do Prawn holds great danger for you."

"If I would get the belt, then I must return there," I said slowly. "And if the gift of moly does not hold long enough—" I drew a deep breath as I surveyed the withered sprig within the globe, "then it is as a pard I must go."

His steady gaze met mine. There was that in his yellow eyes which—

"You are the snow cat!"

He neither nodded nor spoke his affirmation of my discovery. But I knew that was true.

"But—" I glanced down at the belt about his jerkin. Its strap was the common one of tanned leather that any man would wear. "You have no belt." I made a statement of that, not a question. "Then how—?"

Now he did shake his head. A rule of the Power stood between us, I understood, just as I began to know why these three had not named names in my hearing. The oldest rule of all is: a name is not to be given to a stranger, lest he make use of it in some ensorcellment. That I had anything to fear from the Star Tower, I was sure was not so. But that those within it would not give me shelter to their own peril, that I thought was also true.

"The Shadow gathers strength." He broke the silence between us with words that had no immediate meaning for me. "Those who have taken the Darker Way awake, prepare to fare forth once more. I have a question concerning this Ibycus, the trader. You felt nothing in him of the Dark?"

I shook my head. "Rather, he seemed otherwise. Almost I wondered if he was some messenger or scout for the Voices."

"The Voices, now there is a thought that bears shifting." His hand lay on the hilt of his long hunter's knife, drawing it a fraction from the sheath, then sending the blade thudding back into hiding once again. "Perhaps there approaches a time when once more we of Arvon must choose sides. Short indeed has been our peace."

There was a set to his lips, his weary eyes were now half-veiled beneath their lids. In this moment, the illusion of youth that he wore so well slipped a little and I thought he had perhaps seen long years of time in Arvon.

"And," he swung about to face me squarely, "to play small games with the Power in such a time is to invite peril beyond reckoning. I do not like it that winged eyes, which might be servant to your Wise Woman, circle now above this Tower!"

There was determination in that, a threat if I wished to read it so. Without any farewell, he went out—while I still sat upon the bed, holding in my hand the moly that had given me respite from the curse, wondering how much longer the respite might last.

After the man had left, I glanced about me, more interested now in the room than I had been when those three were in it. The odd shape, with one wall striking out in a point to help fashion the star space, made it strange. The walls were unbroken by any pictures or hangings such as the Keep chambers had. There was the bed upon which I lay, a narrow, shelflike affair. Against one wall a chest, richly carven, against the facing wall a small table on which rested a jug and washing basin. Poor looking indeed.

Yet herein I felt a kind of oneness such as I had never experienced in the Keep. There were signs of age about the walls, even as that which clung like moldering tapestry to the walls of Car Do Prawn. But here was not an age that made me feel the insignificant intruder, rather, in a strange way, one with all about me.

That I should have this sensation, in a place where manifestly I was not welcome, was strange. I had no training in the Power, no talent for it. And this was clearly an abode, even a fortress, steeped in the forces that very few of us can understand. Why then did I feel as if I never wanted to leave the Tower?

I got to my feet. Strength flowed back. I could bend and twist my body, as I did in test, and feel no pain from my back. When I quested with my fingers as best I might, crooked my neck as far as I could, to see my wounds, they showed pink, coated with new skin, well along to complete healing. So healed, I had no right to call for any more shelter. The hawk above was a warning of that. I wanted to bring no ill upon the ones who had succored me, even though they considered me unworthy.

It was the last thought that I chewed upon bitterly. The utter indifference of the Moon Witch clung as an irritating memory in my mind. Why did I long, above all else, to stand well in her sight? That was as utter folly as to expect any tenderness from Thaney! I must set aside such fantasies.

I—

As quickly as my man form had been reborn, so now it went from me. The globe I had kept in my hand dangled loosely, to slide from a paw that could not cup it. Four-footed, furred, I was once more the pard. Within the globe, the sprig of green was dark, completely withered.

A growl from the door whipped me about. One of the wild cat cubs snarled at me, the other hissed. The Moon Witch and her pets had returned.

She did not seem startled at my change. Perhaps she had already guessed that the moly had ceased to hold back the curse. The sooner now I was out of the Star Tower, into the forest—

For the first time I saw her expression soften, her lips curve into a smile that brought a whine from me. For, in that moment, all my hard-built wall against her indifference was overthrown. She put down the fur-ridged cub who withdrew, spitting and hissing.

Then she stooped and drew off the chain that held the globe.

"Listen." Her fingers touched my head lightly. I could still feel the touch upon my fur even as she withdrew her hand. "You wish to go—that is well. But there is another key besides the belt. We cannot tell it to you, that is the geas—the command to be fulfilled—that enwraps it. If you can learn that secret, then you shall be far greater than you believe. Now—I may say no more, by the Power I hold in my small portion. I only trust that you shall find your key!"

She stood aside as I brushed past her. There was a door not too far away. Through that I flashed, so into the open, running between the highly scented herb beds, the fringe of the forest before me. It was not until I reached the shade under the first of the trees that I looked back at the Star Tower.

I half expected to see the hawk circling above it. But

the sky was empty. However, though it was still day, from
the poles I had seen as dim torches by night, there now
wreathed that which was not light but more like the
smoky clouds born of Ursilla's ceremonial braziers. Watching the gathering wisps of cloud, I padded back. My test
proved the truth of what I had believed. I could not now
pass the barrier. The disturbing element that had been
caused by my presence was gone. Once more those who
had undoubtedly saved my life and given me, if only for
a short time, relief from the curse, were behind their wall
of protection.

If I longed to remain within sight of the Tower, I knew
such lurking was of no use. Their defenses would not drop
for me again. Perhaps if I could, by some unbelievable
miracle, regain my man form once more, be Kethan,
untied to any plot of Ursilla's, then I could come hither
and find the barrier down. But such a hope was very faint.

However, the words of my Moon Witch (how I longed
to know her name!) were fresh in my mind. Both she
and the Wereman who had saved my life had hinted that
there was another way, besides the belt, besides the short-
lived moly, to achieve shape-change. I was no sorcerer
and they must know it, for the Power can never be
hidden from another who possesses it. Thus they would
not have said that had they thought I could not find the
answer for myself.

I must set myself now to do so, though I had no scrap
of knowledge at the moment to aid me. However, if
Ursilla's hawk was cruising, then I needs must first find
a good hiding place beyond the reach of its keen eyes
before I turned my mind to the riddle the ones in the
Star Tower had set me.

Of the Discovery I Made and How I Planned to Put It into Use

Having no better place to go I drifted again to the streamside, fed on an unwary fish, then hunted out a hiding place among the rocks, one that could not be viewed from the air. Coming hither I had kept under cover, hoping that no airborne spy might sight me.

Always in my mind was the puzzle those of the Tower had set me. They were not malicious of spirit, trying to delude me. If they believed there was a way that one could win back to one's proper shape, then it existed. The man who had been the snow cat wore no belt. However, that he was Wereborn was entirely possible.

Must I search out such a plant as the moly? The sheer impossibility of such a quest daunted me so, I would not long consider the suggestion. Some ceremony then—? But how could that be so? Only those tutored in the Power dared call upon any manifestation of it.

Over and over I repeated in my mind the last words of the Moon Witch. There was a key—and, if it did not exist outwardly, then—within! Within myself! Did it hint that I possessed talent and did not know it? But if so— would Ursilla not have detected that early? Or—

Back my memory flashed to the strange time when the Wise Woman and my mother wrought over me some spell, on the eve that I was to leave their custody for another's. Suppose Ursilla *had* sensed some portion of talent in me and thus made sure that it would be quenched or imprisoned by the spell they wove around me that night?

Sorcery was a matter of learning, though one had to have a measure of inborn talent to fuse with the learning before using it to any advantage. A man or woman might steep mind and memory in the wisdom laid up in ancient runes and yet be unable to put this into use. Still— Ursilla in the days of her teaching me had selected only certain rune rolls for my reading. Others were kept under lock and key, fast shut within her chests. Had the forbidden records held what she feared for me to learn? The more I considered the idea, the more my suspicion grew that I had been deliberately kept from any knowledge that could have provided me the means of freedom.

Whether I possessed any talent or not, it now remained that those of the Tower believed I could free myself from the curse of a pard's body, *if* I found the right way to attempt such a feat. Upon their opinion I began to rely.

Nothing outside myself. More and more did I incline to the truth of that. The answer lay within my mind, entrapped there perhaps by Ursilla's meddling, or maybe only unused because I had never thought it could exist.

Who was I? To those of the Keep, I was Kethan, heir to Erach. To Ursilla and my mother, I was their way to power. To Maughus, Thaney, the Lady Eldris, I was a barrier between them and what they wanted—that same power. To all there, I was not really a person, but a thing that could help or hinder their own desires. What did any of them care that I might have wishes or desires of my own?

The belt—why had Ibycus brought it? I was firm in my belief now that the trader (who could be more than a trader) had had a reason to carry that into Car Do Prawn. Who *was* Ibycus and why did he wish to meddle with my destiny?

Perhaps I was now reading far too much into the short exchange between us in the early morning. Yet, when I summoned up that picture from memory, it remained firm, well set. There had been no taint of the Shadow about the trader. My mother had hinted that he had had some dark purpose in selling the belt to the Lady Eldris, to my harm. I believed not. What he had said to me had been a promise, not a warning of any evil.

Therefore—the belt had more reason than just to make me Ursilla's tool. Its promise of freedom was not a lie but the truth. Only, I did not have the belt.

Back I returned to the hard fact that if there was a key, I did not know it, could not hope to find it without some hint as a guide.

I lay blinking out at the rocks and the river. Once or twice I tensed as wings swept the air above. Neither time did the flyer have the appearance of Ursilla's fierce servant. A key—within—

My nature was now dual as I had early discovered. There was the man part that could think ahead, plan, hope and despair. And, there was, to counter that, the pard who moved by instinct, had flares of rage or hunger, whose intelligence followed other patterns. Suppose— suppose the key lay in those other patterns?

Dared I allow the man to sink wholly into the pard without a battle? I shrank from that. The fear of being lost, man within beast, was strong in me. But if I were to find that key—I must search, not the land without, but what twisted, hidden ways lay within myself.

Now I deliberately forced the man to meet the pard, to sink into the animal, as I lay in my hiding hole. Down, down, past the layer of the hunting instinct, the fighting, defensive part, down, deeper and deeper. That which was Kethan was caught in a maze of thought totally strange to man—lost in the ways not understood. Yet Kethan went deeper still.

The man reached a point about which swirled a trap. To remain here—no! A struggle to break free, to emerge. I waged such a fight as no physical action could ever equal. Up—up—and out! As a drowning man fights to reach the surface of water, fill his aching lungs once more with the air he must have, so did the identity of Kethan reach toward the outer part of the mind, the identity he had so invaded. Up and out!

I lay panting in great gasps as if I had indeed been engaged with an enemy. But Kethan was once more in command. What I had sought did not lie in the depths of the pard mind. That I now knew, almost to my undoing. Therefore, it must be within Kethan.

How could I seek it within myself? Might I reverse the process—let the pard mind search for me, as an animal noses out the trail of a quarry? But that I did not know how to do. What I had found within the beast—the vigorous energy, the patience of the feline hunter, the will to defend threatened territory—the instincts of life— they all added up to a force as strong as a man's will—if I could draw upon them without releasing the pard identity.

Memory was not going to serve me, that I already knew—not memory that could be drawn upon consciously. Did I have also an unconscious memory that held more, far more, than I was aware of?

I drew a mind picture of a room in which there were tall standing presses of rune rolls, all clasped together. Each of them held some portion of memory. Which one must I now take into my hand and open for enlightenment?

My mental picture grew stronger, sharper as I bent all my will and desire on forming it. Slowly, cautiously I tapped the energy of the pard's fierce nature, drawing more strength to back my will. This was *so*—the rune rolls of my mind lay spread so before me. It remained for me to choose the right one, to open and read.

I was deep caught in my picture. That which was Kethan moved between the lines of presses as a man might walk through a material room. Here and there I paused, still never did there come to me the spark that said this was the right one, the choice I must make. Had I mistaken my course? Fiercely, I thrust the weakening thought away. No, somewhere here the knowledge lay— it must be found!

More and more I drew upon the pard, brighter, more real became the room, sharper and sharper the runes that identified the rolls. I was going far back in memory. Then, before me, was a dark shadow leaning ominously across the space through which Kethan must move. This I knew to be the bar Ursilla had set to imprison me.

Kethan alone could not summon the force to cross it. But Kethan and the pard—yes! It was as if I were engulfed knee-high in a sucking horror of a bog through which I might push only a finger-wide space at a time. Still I fought forward, the pard giving me the force of will to win. Then—the bar lay behind me. Something was in this part of my sealed-off memory—something that was a threat to Ursilla. Therefore, it could well be the key I thought. Which roll—where—?

On an on—and as my search was prolonged, so did my hope begin to fade. The picture rolls grew fewer on the shelves of the presses. What memories could lie in my very early childhood that would have any importance now?

I came to the last of the presses—three volumes only. But—my hand (so did I think of myself as *in* that room) went out to the last volume. I drew it out of hiding, opened it—

There was only a picture within—but it was clear, laid in brilliant color. A pard's body on the ground, a man arising from its head, and in his eyes—Now—I *knew!*

I released the mind picture of the room, the energy of the pard, I withdrew from memory. Now I lay outstretched, too weak to lift my furred head from the rock under me, as worn of body as if I had journeyed leagues without rest. But I had won!

It remained now to see if I could use the knowledge I had found. But not at once. I was too wearied by the search. Twilight was closing in. Nor was my small world unpopulated at that moment. So deeply had I been sunk in my search that I had not been warned by my outward senses. However, I could see clearly, riding at a purposeful trot along the bank of the stream, nearing my hiding place, a man.

Also—one I had seen before. It was he who wore the eagle helm, had held converse silently with the snow cat near this same place. His horse was surefooted amid the loose gravel of the stream shore, and the rider held the reins loosely, as if to leave for his mount a choice of path.

The closer he drew to me, the farther I shrank back into my crevice. For, though his meeting with the snow cat had been a friendly one, that did not mean the stranger might see in me anything but a dangerous beast. Nor had I any reason to wish to attract his attention.

I tried to make out the features under the shadow of the helm, though, even to my cat's sight, they were hard to see. There was a haunting resemblance in what I could distinguish, but it was not until he passed me by that I realized from whence the feeling of familiarity had come.

This bird-crested rider was much like the man of the Tower—Another Were?

The rattle of hooves in the gravel, the faint sound of chain mail scraping against saddle, stilled. I dared to creep out of my hole, gaze downriver. The mount had waded out into the shallow stream, was crossing in the direction of the Tower. I hunched down to watch the helm safely out of sight.

I killed before night came, a slow-moving creature I could not set name to, something I had not seen before. It was much like a house lizard, yet many times the size of one of those small reptiles. And it had a brightly colored tail, which my pard nature distrusted, so that I devoured only half the body.

My strength was returning. I needed only to test myself. Then I knew well what I must do. If I had indeed learned the key, entering the Keep must be attempted. For I could not be ever sure of freedom until I had the belt once more. And to go into the very heart of what I now considered enemy territory was something that must be well planned.

The moon was waning this night. The strong influence that had kindled the shape-change in me would be failing. I could not choose better to test its temporary defeat.

Under the waning moon, on top of the rocks, I began my struggle. Just as I had fought to regain memory, now I turned within my mind to the building of the conception of Kethan as he was—a man! More and more detailed grew that picture. Finally, I held it finished and firm. So Kethan *was!*

Truly this was like forcing a key to turn in the lock of a stubborn door. Then—

The night wind was cold about my bare body, which now was not provided with a coat of fur. I stood, throwing my arms high toward the moon, so exultant in my triumph that I could have shouted aloud. But my moment of man-life was not long. I could not hold the change upon the first endeavor for longer than several deep breaths. Once more I was the pard.

Only—I had done it! This I knew was the secret of the Werekin. How such change had been granted to one not of their blood and birth—that I could not tell. But that I might master the pard for periods of time I now understood. I must draw upon my inner forces, harness the beast to the wishes of the man, until I could bring about such a change long enough to penetrate the Keep. Ursilla and Maughus would expect the animal. I would deal with them in human form where they dared try neither to master nor kill me, lest they evoke the ancient penalty for kinhurt.

However, I was still far from mastery of change to the point where I would have time enough to do what I must within Car Do Prawn. Time might be very short, yet I dared not allow that thought to push me into unconsidered action.

Thus began my self-schooling. I lay in hiding during the day, but, at night, as the moon lessened, I would turn my key—and the power to stand as Kethan grew each time I marshaled it to my service. I believed that with the coming of complete dark of the moon I could be ready to attempt Car Do Prawn. Thus I moved through the forest toward the Keep, hiding by day, ranging at night.

That all was not peaceful under those great trees could, I was sure, be sensed by any who penetrated only a short way into that unknown. I did not meet any of the forest people, and I had made a wide circle to avoid the Star Tower, since I knew that it was closed to me, even if I had found my own mastery of form. However, there were stirrings, comings and goings, which were to be felt rather than seen or heard. I did not know whether it was the pard's more-than-human senses that recorded this, or if I was now more fully attuned to any manifestation of the Power.

There were places that I avoided with an inward shrinking. And it appeared to me that they grew more numerous every night, as if some seed of evil had been planted, sprouted, now grew outward, to encompass more and more about it. On my first flight into the depths of the woods I had not been aware of them at all.

Perhaps the inflow of the tide of the Shadow that Pergvin had spoken of now gained momentum. If so, the dark of the moon would feed it. For the Shadow grows ever in the dark, and to *it* light is a burden or even a blow.

I reached the fields before nightfall on the evening that I knew I must make my entrance. My unease had been greatly increased by this strangeness in the forest. Tonight it seemed that, with the setting of the sun, twilight loosed upon the fields a threat.

Lights winked, too early by far, in the houses of the village, the windows of the Towers. I noted that with new dismay. It would be almost certain that there would be sentries at the Gate. I could not walk boldly in, even were I again a man. Also, I must have clothing.

There was a shepherd's hut not too far from the edge of the woods. Toward that I slunk. I had already noted one unusual thing about the Keep. No Lord's banner crackled in the breeze from the tip of the great Tower, which meant that Lord Erach was not under the roof this night.

Dimly, as if it had been voiced a year ago, I remembered the talk of a muster of forces at the Keep of our High Lord, the coming together of the Redmantle Clan. I had not counted the days I had spent in the forest—the day of summons might have already arrived. Would the absence of many of the garrison make my task any easier? Would not those who remained be even more alert?

I sniffed the crack of the hut door. Sheep—a man—but both scents were stale. When I inserted my claws in the crack and exerted my strength the door came open.

The single, bare room was empty. Fortune spread wide wings over me, for there was a shaggy sheepskin coat hanging from a hook in the wall—such as a shepherd wore in the winter months when he must bring the flock into snugger quarters in a fold.

This night the dark was thicker, or was that only because I wished it so? I tried not to let my desires deceive me. At last I brought my will to bear, and Kethan stood in the hut.

With the shepherd's long fleeced coat about me, I made my way to the Keep, rounding its wall well under the shadow of the Towers. There was a sentry at the Gate, well enough. And the man was alert, looking into the dark as one who expects, that at any moment, the enemy may materialize before his eyes.

I hunched my shoulders. To attack the man, perhaps that I could do. I could even lapse into the pard's shape. But I might not strike down the innocent doing his duty. For it came to me that if I shed blood in this fashion, then I was lost. The beast's way must not be mine.

To have reached this point and then to fail was more than I could bear, yet I could see no way out. While I hesitated, my frustration growing, that sense of mine, which was ever aware of the emanations from the forest was set alert. Only—it was not evil that threatened, it was Power working.

As I watched, completely shaken, I saw the sentry stiffen, his eyes fix and focus on a point, become rigid as he stood. Whence came that which reduced him to something that was no longer a threat, I did not know. But I took advantage of it, slipping past into the courtyard.

Behind me I heard movement. I crouched and whirled, ready to face a sword's point. But, though the man moved again, his back was to me, his head did not turn. He had roused out of the trance perhaps without knowledge that he had ever been so neglectful of his duty.

Why? My first relief became the glimmering of suspicion. Though I had not known that force to be of evil, yet it came too readily to my aid. I had no friend to serve me so.

Ursilla!

That I must face her I had somehow known. Only I was not the green youth she had so overborne before. Since I had learned the pard's ways and gone back to my first thoughts, I had become another. And by keeping guard— Though never must I underestimate the Wise Woman.

"Welcome back, Kethan."

I was not astonished this time. That Ursilla was a shadow stirring within the shadows of the Tower arch was only what I should expect. As a duelist might approach the field of engagement, so I walked to where she stood.

Before I had reached her, she slipped around the edge of the doorway. I caught a dim gleam of lamp beyond. Now I had no recourse but to follow. Where Ursilla was, there would be the jargoon pard. And as yet, I had no plan of how to deal with her. Bargain I would not—

As I came within the Tower, I saw her on the stairs. She held a lamp in her hand, the light from which spread thinly to fall upon me. I saw her eyes widen a fraction as if she had not expected to see Kethan. Had she not sighted me in the courtyard, or had I only been a form she had known through the talent?

Her other hand moved. Within its grasp was her wand —a length of bone carved and inlaid with runes, red and black. I guessed she made sure that I saw it, just as Maughus in the same kind of confrontation would have made certain I sighted a bared sword, a ready weapon.

"Greeting, Wise Woman." I spoke for the first time.

Her hand was stretched a little forward as if both to see and hear the better. She made a sharp gesture with the wand.

I felt within me the rise of the pard. Now I did not try to withstand that engulfment. Ursilla must not yet learn what I knew. If she would test my shape-control, let her believe it was slight. I must gather my force of will and hoard it against a time when a single, strong thrust perhaps could save me.

Thus as a beast, I followed her, silent-footed up the stairs.

Of How I Was Prisoner to Ursilla and My Mother Foretold My Future

Only when I was safely in Ursilla's outer chamber did she turn to face me once again. Three lamps burned here beside the small one she had carried in her hand. In the light of those we were fully revealed to one another. Ursilla was smiling.

"Have you learned then, Kethan, that I am not one to be denied?" she asked slowly. She might be relishing each word as a man relishes some flavor or a favorite dish not too often set before him on the dining board.

I had never denied her Power, I thought. But human speech was now lost to me.

The Wise Woman seated herself in the room's single chair, one as regal as those that my mother and the Lady Eldris held right to. Slowly she surveyed me, from head to tail tip and back again. There was satisfaction in her face. I could feel her confidence, not only in her own talent, but in what might lie before her that she had me once more to hand.

"Twice were you summoned," Ursilla continued. "And in your folly you came not. For that there must be proper punishment in its own time. But first—"

Once more she pointed at me with the tip of her wand. I cried out in answer, for I felt then as if the rod had reached inside me, prodded and tore at my throat. I gagged, saliva dripped from my jaws.

Ursilla leaned forward, her eyes holding mine. "Do you understand, Kethan? I can mold you—answer me!"

So sharp was her order that my tongue and throat worked.

"I—understand—" The words were ill-spoken, for they had been shaped by a part of my pard form that was never intended to voice human speech. Yet they could be understood.

She nodded briskly. "Well enough! Now you shall answer me— What Power came between us when last we met?"

She meant the time of my journey in the Shadow land. But—and this I was now sure of—unlike the snow cat she could not speak mind-to-mind. If so, she would not have meddled to give me the ability to answer aloud. Therefore, it should follow that she could not read my mind either. I could pick and choose the words of my answer, giving enough of the truth to satisfy her, but not all.

"When—you—called—" It was very difficult to mouth human speech, and my throat began to ache from the effort. "I—was—in—edge—place—of—Power had defense—used it to break—contact between us—"

"A place of Power," Ursilla repeated. "There are such in the forest, some long forgot. Of what manner was this place you discovered?"

I dared not tell her of the Star Tower, or even of the clearing wherein grew the moonflowers. Though I had found no refuge there, those dwelling within had assuaged my hurts. And the snow cat had saved my life (perhaps more than just the life of my body), when he had broken the web of the lurker. The ruin! It would do no harm to give her the ruin!

"Two pillars—old carvings on them—but nigh worn away— They guard a ruin—the blocks so tumbled—I could—not—tell what manner of place it was—"

The wand swung again in her hand and I felt a queer pain between my eyes. That she was in some manner judging the truth I spoke, I understood. I felt a heavy burden of unease lest she could still drag from me what I determined not to disclose.

"Truth it is between us. Later you shall tell me more of this place. If, even though a ruin, it has Power to break the door spell, then it must have soaked up much might of some great talent in the past. Was it also the place that gave you the semblance of man again, Kethan?"

"Yes."

I braced myself for another testing. What would she do when she found *that* answer a lie? However, to my overwhelming relief, she was disposed to accept my answer without prying into its truth.

"Power indeed! Surely must we find the place!" The fingers of the hand that did not hold the rod crooked as if she would grasp some treasure. Then she sighed. "But that must wait another day. As for you, shape-changer—" She gave me again her full attention. "You shall do as I bid. My messenger, who left his marks across your loins, did very well. I hold the belt. And there are various things that can be accomplished through it—as you shall discover if you try to stand against my will!"

Her cold voice held no idle threat, but deadly promise. The worst of my burden was that I could not be sure whether or not she was right. Could I, within range of her Power, use my key and put on my proper shape, even for a short time? I had no answer to that until I tried. And I must not risk such a trial until I was sure that it was the only manner of defense left me.

"Maughus commands the Keep since the Lord Erach has ridden with most of the men to the ingathering," Ursilla continued. "He has had silver bolts forged since his first hunting failed, and he has sworn to bring you down. Nor will any here lift hand or voice to gainsay him. For all fear the coming of the Shadow and it was very easy for him to argue that a shape-changer in our midst is an open door for worse things. He moves—" She stopped, biting her lower lip between her teeth as one who betrays too much.

I believed that I could supply the end of the sentence she had enough prudence not to complete. Maughus moved also against Ursilla. However, I did not think him wise in that. Having had a goodly taste of what she could summon to aid her in her desires, I knew that my cousin would have little chance if he turned Ursilla openly against him. Were I he, I would be more than a little cautious of how I went—for Ursilla threatened was a peril few men would care to reckon with.

"Only here are you safe," she said, with no change in her features, though that fact gave her satisfaction to point out, I knew. "You have no friends herein, Kethan. Your fair betrothed," her smile now was gloating, "has broken the bond between you, and her father did not gainsay her in that, having the testimony of those who hunted a pard from these walls."

"If Lord Erach—" I forced the words from my maltreated throat, "has so spoken, what manner of use am

I now to you? For never will they shield-raise me as his heir—"

Her pinched smile did not lessen. "Not so. What sorcery has wrought, sorcery can mend. I have sworn that you shall be restored to your proper person—and that you shall, if you obey me. Then will I govern—"

That she need not complete either. I could well do it for her. If she restored me from what she proclaimed to be a curse laid upon me by the Lady Eldris working with Maughus, then her position would be very strong. Not only would she be properly feared for the Power she wielded, but I must be slave to her who might return me at whim to beast shape. Yes, Ursilla's place in the Keep was assured—*if* she could keep me alive and out of Maughus's hands, *if* she could defeat the belt and make me wholly human.

At that moment, I knew I did not want my body back at the price Ursilla would place upon such a bargain. I had known for many seasons that she stood behind my ambitious mother with plans of her own. Now all my suspicions were fully confirmed. It would be Ursilla who ruled here if I was shield-raised, the Lord Erach dead.

"Now"—she rose from her throne, snapped her fingers at me as a man summons the attention of a hound—"we shall keep you secret for a while. Also, I have that to do which will reveal the future, that I may lay my plans well based and prepared against all eventualities."

So summoned, I followed her meekly into the inner chamber where lay the star painted on the floor. Into the center of the star I went, when she pointed to me with the wand. Then, she raised the symbol of Power and indicated with it each of the candles set in the points. They blazed up though no fire had been touched to them.

"Safe," she commented. "None can come at you here, nor can you fare forth, shape-changer. Thus you shall remain awaiting my future pleasure."

She turned and left me, while the candles burned with

a steady flame. Crowding in upon me (for the star might have been filled with unseen bodies jostling in a throng), was the sense of Power unleashed.

So far I had made but a sorry showing in my own attempt to win free from Ursilla. She had the belt, and there were half-a-hundred places within the Keep where it might be concealed. Here I was pent and unable to hunt. What did I have? Only the strength that I had earned to make me man again for intervals that were all too far short.

I prowled around the altar of stone set in the middle of the star—the one on which my mother had laid me on the long ago night when Ursilla had set her guard upon my mind. My mother? Did she know I had returned to Car Do Prawn? Or was she now so submissive to Ursilla that the Wise Woman saw no reason for sharing with the Lady Heroise any part of what she believed I could gain here?

However, the relationship between the two was of little importance to me now. What mattered was that Ursilla had me pent with her sorcery. I advanced cautiously toward the nearest portion of the star drawing. A paw put out to the line brought about the same shock that I had felt when I tried to enter the garden at the forest Tower.

The Star Tower! I sat back on my haunches. As the Moon Maid had urged, I had sought and found the key, though I was still unsteady and limited in the use of it. Could—could the same key apply not only to the control of my shape, but other things? Might my will be turned outward to defeat the barrier Ursilla had set around me?

I could—

But I was to have no time, for the door of the chamber opened and in came my mother, her richly bordered robe sweeping the floor, her eyes seeking me out. Like Ursilla, she was smiling. There was no mirth in her smile, only pleasure in my state of prisoner.

"You have gone your way, fool," she said as she paused between two of the star points' candles, their stiffly upstanding, unbending flames awaking a glitter from her collar neckace, her girdle, the gems at her ears caught in the net about her hair, on her fingers. She was dressed as one bound for a high feasting. "And how has it served you?"

I would not try to croak an answer in the half-voice Ursilla had forced upon me. There was no use in adding pleasure to her delight in seeing me so imprisoned.

The Lady Heroise laughed. "You—*you* are trying to pit yourself against our Power! Did you think you had a chance?

Our Power, she had said. But I believed that Ursilla would not agree to that. If my mother was so deceived as to think the Wise Woman was only her handmaid in my subduing, then perhaps a hint of the truth might set a useful wedge between them. I did find my voice:

"Ursilla brought me." I got out the words with difficulty. "She would use me. Nothing was said of you—"

Her smile did not alter. "Ursilla is very strong, Kethan. But just perhaps—not as all seeing, all performing, as she would like us to think. We do not quarrel now, for our purpose is the same."

With her usual grace, she turned from between the candles to approach a table above which hung a single lamp. To this she pointed as Ursilla had done, to start a flame leaping there. I think with this small gesture she wished to show me that she, too, could command some forces, though such tricks were among the lesser of any talent.

There were no throne-backed chairs here, only a three-legged stool such as might be found in a villager's kitchen. It was carved and much timeworn. My mother seated herself thereon, and took up, from where it dangled on a chain from her belt, a box that I could see—even through the haze the flame set about it—was covered with runes.

She slipped off its lid with long-practiced ease and spilled out into her hand a pack of cards made from stiffened parchment. I knew them for her greatest treasure, for such aided in foretelling. They were not generally used among our people. It was said that they were not of the Power of Arvon at all, but one of the tools that those who had opened Other World Gates in the past had drawn through for service here. They were seldom put into use as there were few learned in reading any message they had to tell.

That my mother could do so was her great pride. At Garth Howel, this much talent had she shown, rather confounding those who had instructed her in the mysteries, for she was not otherwise greatly endowed. Now her smile grew brighter as she looked upon them in her grasp.

"Unfortunately, Kethan, you cannot shuffle or cut these as you should, having not the hands to do so. But this day and hour is the proper one for a reading and I shall keep you in mind as I do this."

She had flipped swiftly through the cards and now chose one that she held up to let me view the picture it bore. "This will stand—or rather lie—for you. It is the Page of Swords, being a youth surrounded with a certain strength."

This she laid upon the table. Now her fingers moved gracefully and skillfully, shuffling the cards once, cutting them with her left hand three times in my direction, shuffling again, cutting again, and then once more shuffling. She paid no more attention to me as she did this, the expression on her face one of intense concentration. I found myself as intent upon what she would do next as if indeed I hung across the board opposite her, believing that she could read what would chance for me in days to come.

Now she laid the cards out in a circle, beginning to

the left, moving downward, then up to complete the round. She seemed not to look at them until she was through. Then, when she pushed aside those she did not use, she bent over the twelve on the board with the same fixed concentration.

"The Devil in the First House—that House that is yours. Ah—" She drew a deep breath. "Bondage—Magic for you— The Two of Wands in your House of Property —Lord of the Manor—Fortune—dominance—

"The Third House—there lies the Moon—peril—dreams— The Four of Wands for your Fourth House—coming of peace and perfected work—a haven of refuge—" As she spoke, her voice quickened, her face revealed shadows of emotion I could not read.

"In the Fifth House, the Ace of Wands—a birth—yes, the starting of Fortune—an inheritance—true, all true!" With her fingertips she drummed lightly beneath each card as she revealed the meaning it held for her.

"For the Sixth House—success—prudence—safety—!" With each reading her voice arose a little, her excitement grew more plain. "The House of Seven—here lies the Six of Swords, which means passage from difficulties—success after anxiety—

"Now the Eighth House—wherein lie your nature gifts— The Magician!"

She sat staring at the card for a long moment, puzzlement replacing the satisfaction she had earlier expressed. "Mastery of skill, of wisdom, the ability to direct Power through desire into manifestation— But how can that be! Ah, such cannot be meant for you. No, of course, you are the tool through which others shall work." But I do not think she wholly believed the quick answer to the problem that her previous cards had shown her. While in me, for the first time, grew a truer interest in what she was saying.

The ability to take Power from above, direct that through desire into manifestation. Was that not exactly what I had learned in my shape-changing? But if it had been a true reading, then what of the rest she had so lightly foretold—success—peace? If I could only believe that they were true!

"The Ninth House." My mother swept on as if she wished to leave the troublesome eighth card well behind her. "Five of Wands— Ah, this is truth—struggle to obtain success—loss—unless there is vigilance. But we shall be vigilant! Of that there is no doubting.

"Now—the Eleventh House—what lies there? Seven of Swords—a plan that may fail—uncertainty. Again a warning, and one we little need. Last of all—the Twelfth House—the Hierophant—ruling Power of belief, the need to be one with others—"

She raised her hands from the table, no longer regarding the cards, but watching me across the candles in the star points.

"You see the truth in this, Kethan? There lie great things ahead for your grasping. The way shall be hard, but no path to rulership is ever easy. You are told to be wary, but you are promised success, a oneness with others. It is a good reading— Still—" Once more she looked at the card she named the Magician lying in the Eighth House. "This I do not quite understand. Ah, well, ofttimes some parts of any foreseeing lie hid. The rest is all correct within my knowledge. You shall rule in Car Do Prawn yet, my son, and perhaps even beyond this single holding—"

She gazed over the cards to the wall, her expression that of one lost in some splendid fantasy of imagining. Twice she nodded in answer to her thoughts, not to any speech. Then she swept the cards swiftly together, restored them to their case, arose from the table.

"Be glad that Ursilla has left you safe," she said as she turned toward the door. "Maughus has had silver bolts forged, he swears within his heart to bring you down—

and silver is the death for any shape-changer when it is weapon wrought. Let him lord it here while yet he can. His day shall be a short one."

I heard the whisper of her fine skirts across the floor, then she was gone. But her foretelling had left me with several thoughts. Now I tried to remember each card, the message she had gained from it. I would not have been so impressed had I not been struck by the answer she had read from the Magician, that which had puzzled her so. Master of skill and wisdom—I was very far from that. There were such—one heard tales of them—the Voices, others, some of the Dark, some of the Light. But they dwelt apart and one might not see one in a long lifetime —nor even meet another human who had seen one!

Restlessly, I paced around the altar block. I felt no hunger or thirst, nor was I tired. Perhaps some virtue within the wall Ursilla had erected kept me from such bodily discomforts. Only I could not practice patience and wait. I wanted to be at the action that had brought me back to Car Do Prawn.

Now I began to survey the room with all the keenness of the pard sight. It seemed to me that if Ursilla concealed the belt she would keep it in this place, which was the repository for all her tools of Power. There was a cabinet against the wall, its doors tight shut. Within that were stored the containers of herbs, the various liquids and powders that were used for ensorcellment. But, that was too obvious. Another case near the door held the rune rolls she had never let me touch. Could the belt perhaps be inside one of those? If so, it was as far from me as if it lay on the silver surface of the moon itself!

Back and forth I paced, my impatience like a whip upon me, or a hunger gnawing from within. The candles continued to burn, yet they did not shrink much in size. It must take a long time for their wax to melt. The stale smell of herbs hung heavy, my head ached a little, a vast depression settled upon me slowly but steadily. I could see no success for any save Ursilla. And, to that success, she would make me the sacrifice if she could.

Of How the Three from the Star Tower Took an Interest in My Fate

I do not know just when I recognized depression for an enemy. Perhaps within me, when I had tried and tested the strength I had for controlling my shape, a long dormant part of my mind had partly stirred to life. Had it been strengthened by the foretelling that had so pleased my mother—even though she was puzzled over that single card?

Such speculation did not serve any purpose. My Kethan mind began once more to assume the rulership of my dual nature. I deliberately fought under the restlessness of the pacing pard and stretched out by the altar. Anyone spying upon me there might think that I had surrendered and now waited tamely for whatever Ursilla planned.

That was far from the truth. I was exploring in another fashion than that of the merely physical. First, I studied the candles burning on the star points. That they in some manner controlled the barrier imprisoning me was a thought that grew steadier. Their flame was orange-red. Those colors mixed, related to physical strength of the body and self-confidence. Yes, those were the Magics Ursilla could well draw upon.

What stood against them? As never before my shape-changing, I began to concentrate on the subject of Magic and the Power. Though Ursilla had carefully selected the Chronicles she had permitted me to read, many of the stories therein had dealt in detail with the exploits of men in Arvon when the Lords and Voices had dueled with forces beyond any strength of arm or weapon.

Once more I summoned up the vision of my memory as a library of rune rolls, of vision I had fought so hard to achieve. This time the picture built up far more swiftly and realistically. I was not searching now for the unknown. I was almost sure where lay the material I would review.

Against the red of the body stood—yellow of mind? No—that was not what I searched for now, since yellow employed logic in which I had no learning or skill. What, then, opposed Thaumaturgy—solid learning? Theurgy, which was of the emotions, faith and belief—*Blue!*

Now what would confront that orange shade of self-confidence—overwhelming belief in one's own Powers? Again I sought—

Within the world of nature, man did not create aught but his own image. Or did he? He who dealt with beauty did so humbly, knowing that he was but the tool, not the true maker. He could foster beauty—cherish it. But that which grew from his own efforts—never was it as wonderful as it had seemed before he brought it into being. Therefore, he was always the seeker, never a fulfilled believer who had accomplished the full sum of what he had wished to do.

Green was the Magic of that seeking, lying in all things sprouting from the earth.

Blue and green.

But if I had the answer, how did I now apply it? Where had I ever seen such colors stand for any sign of Power?

My mind picture changed. Once more I crouched at the edge of the Star Tower garden path, stared at the rise of blue-green stone across the lush harvest of the herbs. The Tower held the secret, and I was walled without!

Yet, so deep now was my need that it compelled me to keep the Tower picture in my mind. I strove to imagine myself walking down the path—entering once more into the queerly shaped room where I had lain when those who dwelt there had tended me. In my mind now, I began to picture the room. It had been thus and thus—

Only I could not bring the picture into any focus. Back and forth it rippled, as might the surface of a pool on which water flies were skating. The room—it *was* so!

All my will I pushed into that single effort. But—

This was not the room I had known! There was no bed—nothing as I remembered it. Instead, on the walls were looped strings of shining disks, winking with some inner light of their own. Three people stood within a circle formed of a chain of the same disks, a circle that was broken in five places by a tall standing, bright silver candlestick in which burned a green candle. The flames that showed therefrom were blue and green, even as the walls about.

At my first sighting, the figures within the circle had been misty, ill defined. However, after I gazed at the candle flames and back again, I could see them as clearly as if some intervening veil or curtain had been ripped away.

The—Moon Maid! Upon her, my eyes centered first. Once more she wore her skirt of moon disks, her horned moon pendant. Her body was as silver white as the lines of the circle in which she stood. In her hands was a silver rod, wound about with the moonflowers I had first seen her harvesting.

Beyond her, also facing inward as she did, was the stranger who had worn the Were shape, though now he was a man. His brown body was bare to the waist, and between his hands was the hilt of a bared sword, the point of which rested on the floor. Along its blade ran tiny waverings of light, steely blue.

The third was the woman who had first denied me refuge in the Star Tower and then nursed my wounded body. No longer did she wear the man's clothing I had seen on her, rather an initiate's robe and it was green. About her waist was a binding girdle of vines still bearing unwithered leaves. The same were woven into the braids of her hair, which now hung down her back.

Her wand with its green leaf spearhead was also pointed inward. I could see her lips moving and believed that she was chanting some spell or call to the part of the Power that she could summon or command to her desire.

What moved me then was an overwhelming need to make them aware of me, for I felt as if I stood in that room though outside their charmed circle. And I cried out—

"Look upon me! I am here!"

It was the Moon Witch whose head moved at my silent cry. She spoke, though I could not hear her words, nor did they resound in my head as had those of the snow cat.

The ones with her turned their heads, looked in my direction. I saw amazement on the woman's face, the man half raised his sword. Then the woman's wand came up, the leaf pointed to me. Her lips shaped words.

In this vision or dream, I could *see* the words, if I could not hear them. They were like glittering insects winged in the air, flying toward me. Then they winked out and were gone.

The amazement on her face grew. She looked down hastily at the wand she held. Back and forth the leaf wove some pattern. From her manner, I guessed that the motion was not of her doing, that the wand now acted independently of her will.

She spoke again and the man moved forward. His sword came up—point foremost in my direction. Still I felt no fear. There was about the vision a feeling of rightness, as if I had found my way to some place where I would be welcome. I must only give those before me time to realize that this was so.

The wavering lines upon the sword blade flashed the brighter. They ran, they dripped in tiny, flashing gobbets from the point of the blade. Only for a breath space did the man hold so, then once more the point sank down. He did not look amazed, only thoughtful. Then he nodded to the Moon Witch, and her flowered rod arose.

From the heart of the stone flowers burst other thin, white blooms. They might each be a source of flame as were the candles about us. They flared and died.

It was my belief that I had been tested in some manner, and that their defenses against me had not worked. I felt no fear, no wariness. All I wanted now, and desperately, was their full favor.

"You are here. What would you have of us?" The woman spoke then and her words were in my mind.

"I would call upon the Blue and the Green—those you serve and command. For they are mine—"

The answer I made her came not from my conscious thinking, rather out of the deepest depths of that which was Kethan.

"Give us your name—"

I knew her meaning. The name is the person, in part. For ill-wishing, a name known to the ill-wisher can serve as a bond or a weapon.

Kethan they had called me from my birth. Ursilla could command me by it if she turned to the ways of the Shadow. *Was* I Kethan? For a moment I was entirely uncertain. That name seemed wrong in this hour, as if it was no part of the real me. Yet I had none other to offer.

"I am Kethan."

"Where are you?" she asked secondly.

"Within Car Do Prawn—within the bonds of the Wise Woman's sorcery."

"What do you seek of us?"

"What I can learn, to free myself."

"It would seem you have already learned much," the woman observed, "since you went forth from here."

"I was told there was a key, if I could find it. I searched, and this was what I found—not by the belt but within myself."

The woman nodded. "Well done, Kethan." Her face lost the masklike quality it had always seemed to hold the times when she had looked upon me. "In truth, you have walked a goodly way down a strange road, but not one under the Shadow. I do not understand how you have become destiny-tied with us—that we must learn. But that you have been able to do so while entranced, coming thus to the edge of our summoning, that is proof that we must travel together, at least for a space. So you are caught within a Wise Woman's sorcery." Now she frowned a little as if facing a problem to be solved. "Tell us the manner of the binding about you."

Though I did not now see Ursilla's room behind the eyelids of my closed eyes, rather the center of the Star Tower, I spoke of the candles that blazed and how I believed that they provided the bars for my captivity.

"A longer way have you come down the road than we thought"—the man spoke now—"if you could search for that which will stand against your prison and find it here. If you are loosed from the spell, what then will you do?"

"I must have the belt—"

"That is so." He gave agreement. "With it this Ursilla can keep you at her heel and her bidding. You know where it lies hid?"

"Not yet. Free, I shall learn—"

For the first time then the Moon Witch spoke. "If you have time." And her words were a dire warning.

"I can but try," I answered her.

"We shall give you what time and aid we can." The woman had locked gaze with the man for an instant, as if they so mingled wills and minds. Now she gave me her promise. "Go from us, look to your candles. Use again the key you have found for yourself—"

I opened my eyes. Gone was the chamber wherein the three had stood. I was again within Ursilla's locked star. I turned my head and stared at the flame burning steadily there. Orange—red—but it—must change—

Just as I had reached deep within me, within the pard —for the strength to change my shape, so now I bent the full force of my desire upon this—that blue and green must stand where now blazed the other hues.

Kethan-strength, pard-strength, I summoned, aimed with my will. Up to the limit of that strength I drew— But there was no change in the flames. I—must—do —better—

Harder I strove— Pard-strength, man-strength—those were not—not—

Into me flowed force of which I was now but the channel. I was aware of a mingling—I was Kethan. I was the pard—and—I was others—the three I had fronted in my vision. Different were the currents as they met and surged through me, as different in kind as the persons who aimed them to aid me. Never in my life had I felt so kin-strong as in that moment.

Darker burned the flame—to purple, the color of the

Shadow—? No, it was changing hue, but from the tip down. No longer was it the orange-red. A blue-green surged along the flame itself. Then—the candle was all of the hue, which I hoped would win my freedom.

With a pard's inborn stealth, I crept toward the candle. Had I indeed broken the circling ensorcellment? On—on—

I was out!

The others who had filled me with their force were gone. I could not have held them, but I felt curiously forsaken, bereft, as I was emptied of their presences. There was no time to dwell on such thoughts—I had to regain the belt before Ursilla returned. With it in my possession, she might still be able to threaten me a little, but I had a chance to withstand her.

I padded to the cupboard, clawed open the door. Only what I expected was within—boxes, flasks, some oddities whose use I did not know. Yet most of it gave forth an aura that tingled along my skin, caused the fur on my spine to rise, my ears to flatten against my skull. I had never been so sensitive to things of Power before. But here was a hint that if Ursilla did not stand in the ranks of the Shadow, she had strayed near to the fringe of Darkness in some of her delving into old and perhaps better-hidden knowledge.

I had not expected truly to find the belt within, but this was the first place to search. The only other receptacle in plain sight was the case of rune rolls and to that I went.

Though I had learning (perhaps more than most since I had found a liking for such knowledge in me and fostered it), I could not translate many of the markings on those rolls. Arvon has its secret tongues, those born of the Power through many ages. I judged that most of the library Ursilla had collected was of very old lore.

I could pass over any that were of lesser bulk, for the belt needed a larger roll if it were so concealed. Now I began to paw out any that looked possible, to shake them open, with little care for their age or worth. It had been a good idea that Ursilla would hide it so, but as my search advanced I decided that I had misjudged her slyness. There was no belt concealed here.

With the last of the possible rolls pawed half-open on the floor, I heard the grate of a lock. Snarling, I faced in that direction, even as the door opened.

Ursilla took one step within her inner chamber, stopped short.

Beneath her coif her eyes narrowed. She looked from me to the circle where the blue-green candle still pointed aloft to betray the manner of my escape. Then, as her gaze dropped to the plundered rolls, she began to laugh.

There was no sound in the laughter, though it shook her body, stretched her mouth. The sight of her amusement was to me as a blow across my beast muzzle. All my small knowledge had been wasted, and I had betrayed myself to the point that she would regain even more control over me.

"Your seeking is fruitless, Kethan." She spoke at last. "But did you believe, poor fool, that I would conceal my leash upon you so? I should think after all the years wherein you were my pupil you would learn better. Though"—she stopped, looking beyond me once again to the blue-green candle flame—"perhaps I have undervalued you a little. Now, how did you learn that trick, I wonder? No." She stretched her lips in the wry grimace that she used for a smile. "There is not quite time enough to delve into such a matter now.

"I have some news—my Lord Maughus knows you have entered the Keep. He is searching room by room. Luckily—"

What she might have said then was unvoiced. Someone else moved into the chamber behind her. Ursilla half-turned, but not quickly enough to prevent the entrance of the other.

In the light of the candles the Lady Eldris stood there,

staring at the scene before her as one looks upon some nightmare come out of the night into the day. She raised her right hand and made one of the Power-averting gestures that are common among those without the talent. Sometimes, if backed by a well-endowed amulet, they are effective against the weaker manifestations of the Shadow.

"What sorcery do you?" Her voice was high and shrill as she flung the question at the Wise Woman.

Ursilla still smiled. "I use the Power in service of your House, Lady. Look upon this poor beast—look well!" She pointed to me. "Can you name him?" Her eyes glittered while she watched the Lady Eldris as a hound might look upon some small, defenseless creature in the field. "I think you can put name to him—the more so since you are responsible for his ensorcellment, even though you have no talent. I know why you wrought so, my Lady. But what is done by the Power can be undone. Kethan shall be Kethan again. And in that hour, look to your own safety, Lady. Often a broken spell will recoil upon the head of him or her who had the laying of it, even if not through their own use of Power but through their employment of others who can do so. Would you, yourself, care to run the forest on four feet—furred—with perhaps a hunt up against you?" She had moved toward the Lady Eldris and now she thrust her face very close to that of my grandam.

The Lady Eldris shrank back, her stare now fixed fully on Ursilla's features, her hands held as if she would ward away some danger, yet feared her strength was not enough to so delay an accounting.

"No!" she screamed, trying to run through the door. But there again another stood, and the flames glinted on a blade.

"Maughus!" The Lady Eldris seized upon his arm, clinging to it with a frenzy, though he tried to throw her off and be free to slay me.

That he intended my death I knew. Now I growled,

crouching low. Ursilla swung toward me. She stood back a little, one hand against the wall. Now she began to slip along it, kicking out to free her skirts from the tangle of loosened rolls I had left across the floor. Her hand was at the corner of the case in which they had been stacked.

"Kill!" Her voice cracked at me "Kill or be killed, fool!"

The Lady Eldris screamed, clinging desperately to Maughus, who struggled roughly now to rid himself of her grasp.

"No!" She shrieked again. "She will blast you—with the Power! Maughus—call up the bowmen with the silver darts. Steel will not harm a Were—"

He paused in the struggle. I could read the calculation in his face. But I was not at all sure of the ancient belief. To me, his sword looked very deadly and real. Though silver darts, by all the learning that I had, were even more perilous to such as I.

"Kill!" Ursilla cried again.

With both hands she tugged at the corner of the roll case, which puzzled me, for I could not see why she did not summon to her service some manifestation of her talent. Though it could well be that she had been laid under geas to do no harm to any member of the household that had sheltered her for so long. Such bonds were known.

"Kill!" As she cried that for the third time, the pard broke free, raging within me. I had left only the animal's reaction to the immediate peril to guide me.

Of How I Chose Not the Beast's Way and of the Secret of Ursilla

Kill, Ursilla had bade me. And the rage was unleased within the pard. But, even as I crouched for the spring that would carry me to my enemy, the man stirred once again in my mind. Were I to so kill—yes, that deed would be but another key to lock me inside the beast. Maughus was my enemy, a threat to me—yes. But as such he must be fronted man to man. If I drew his blood with claw and fang, I trapped myself in the wilder breed.

The Lady Eldris was screaming. If Maughus had not called his men to follow him hither, the cries would surely bring them. I saw death dark before me. Still the stubborn core of man within the beast would not loose my body to attack.

I squalled a cat's battle cry, pard nature striving to evade man's control. No creature faces death tamely. Would the steel blade sing in to let free my life? Or, at the last moment, could I indeed strike back?

Only the fact that Maughus must give support to the Lady Eldris perhaps saved me from the final choice. His face a mask of hatred as deep and hot as that of the pard, he edged back, out of the room. For the Lady Eldris was clawing at him, shrieking and crying that he must wait, that he should let his henchmen deal with me.

Backward she jerked and pulled. He could not loose her hold unless he beat her away. Even his anger could not lead him to do that. Now they were both beyond the threshold. I heard a *word* uttered from where Ursilla stood. The door, without any hand laid upon it, clanged shut.

"Why did you not kill?"

I turned my head. Still the Wise Woman tugged at the case that had held the rune rolls. Her whole body was tense with effort as she strove to move the tall set of shelves.

I growled, for I could no longer answer her in words. That part of her spell had failed.

"It is slay or be slain now," Ursilla continued. "Though Maughus has wrought far worse than he knows this day. And Eldris— Ah, there shall be an answer for my Lady also!"

There followed a grating sound that was louder than the clamor from outside the door, which was muffled by the stout portal now closed. I believed those without brought force to knock the wood down. Maughus's men must have arrived.

However, my attention was for Ursilla and what she had done. At long last some hidden catch had responded to her urging, and the whole of the case swung open to form a second door. Ursilla hurried from it back to the cupboard. There, she gathered up the front of her robe, making a clumsy bag into which she tipped boxes and flasks she chose from her store with flying fingers.

Last of all, she caught up her wand of Power. With it she pointed first to me and then to the hidden door.

"In!" she commanded.

That any Keep as old as Car Do Prawn must have its secrets, I had guessed long ago, though I had not had any proof such existed. Ursilla had made good use of her time during the years she had dwelt here, and I did not doubt that she knew exactly where we were going.

The pounding at the outer door grew heavier. Already the latch had given way. It was only Ursilla's spell that held it fast. How long that could last—who knew?

I slipped through the entrance to the secret way, found beyond stairs that led downward. Cramped and narrow was the passage for it must be contained within the wall itself. My furred shoulders brushed stone on either side. There came dim light from behind and I saw that the tip of Ursilla's wand gave forth a limited glow, providing us with a torch by which to see the way, though there was naught here to sight save rough, dark stone and steps endlessly descending.

How far we went I had no way of measuring. But I was certain that shortly we were below the level of the earth outside the Keep. Still the way led down. Now I heard Ursilla's voice, muffled, echoing a little.

"Brave Maughus! He shall beat his way in and find naught. Then will those with him begin to speak of how a Wise Woman can easily escape such blunderers with the use of her Power. They shall look sidewise at Maughus and straightly at any shadow. For a man may dream up wonders and people his world with them until he can believe they come into view full rounded and alive. No, I do not think Maughus shall rest easy this night to come."

She laughed, not soundlessly, but with a rusty, creaky chuckle, which to my ears was worse than any cursing.

"Yes, not easy shall Maughus rest, nor any within this Keep. There shall be that loosed which will trouble them in many ways."

Then the words I could understand ceased, as she began a queer singsong that made my pard's hair rise along the backbone and nearly brought a protesting squall out of me, save that I did not want to draw upon myself at that moment any of her attention. As long as she occupied her talent with some means of making Maughus unhappy, her mind would not turn toward my further subjection.

That she was not pleased when my pard nature had not driven me to attack my kinsman, I knew well. Doubtless, there would be a reckoning over that. From now on she would be suspicious of my every move, uncertain of her control over me, which could lead to such ensorcellment as I would never escape. The journey through the inner core of Car Do Prawn was only a short breathing space between assaults as far as I was concerned.

I began to wonder at the nature of the goal before us. The stairway was so deep now within the earth (we certainly were well below even the level of the storerooms that made up the cellars of the Keep) that I could not imagine where it would end or its purpose. Had this passage been meant for a secret escape in time of trouble, surely it would have had some outlet nearer to the surface of the ground.

Though there appeared air vents within the walls, and though the way felt damp and there was an acrid odor I could not identify, which increased as we went, still there was breathable air. However, the deeper we went, the more I knew that we were coming to one of those places in which Power of a sort had its being.

I could sense neither the evil that marked the core of any Shadow dwelling place nor the peace that radiated from such sites as the Star Tower. This was something else, carrying with it a heaviness of the spirit, as if the weight of untold ages were centering in and burdening one small place.

Ursilla had ceased her singsong chant and moved in silence except for the rustle of her skirts as they brushed the wall. The light from her wand still gave us a faint sight of what lay about us.

Then, when I had begun to believe that the steps would bring us to the fabled Earth Center from which all life was said to stream long ago, they ended in a passageway.

This was a little wider than the stairs, but it also sloped gradually downward. Here the walls were not smooth, but, at intervals, were broken by carven panels. I could see little of the carvings, in the gloom, even given the pard's superior sight. And there was naught in any I did sight that was familiar to me.

Dust had gathered in the pits and grooves of the carvings, just as it lay under our feet. Only there it had been tracked and marked as if we were not the first to come this way since it settled. And ever grew the feeling that this was an alien place, which did not welcome intrusion. It was far older than Car Do Prawn itself, I was now sure, perhaps dating back to the First Age of Arvon before the warring of the Lost Lords. That would put such an age on it as few men could reckon.

"Wait!" Ursilla's voice startled me, I had grown so used to her silence, the silence of this place. "Here I must lead the way."

I squeezed against the wall, allowing her to pass me. She walked firmly, as if our long descent had in no way tired her, even though she also bore the unwieldy burden in her robe. As she pointed her wand nearly on a level before her, its dim light showed that we had come to a carven archway that might be the end of the passage.

Under it we passed and out into an area I thought must be very large, though a velvet darkness hung about us there, just beyond the arm's-length reach of the wand, for its light penetrated no farther. My padded paws whispered on a floor, Ursilla's footwear awoke an echo. Here we had no wall to guide us, yet Ursilla struck straight out into the dark as if she knew our path very well, could see our goal before us.

Here an oppressive sense of alienness was a burden to hang in the mind, to slow one's thoughts. I labored under a weight of fatigue that grew with every step I advanced. Still I tried to probe it, though I knew not how to use the talent. There was no emanation of evil, nor of what we had come to think of as *good*. This was a Power place, yes, but of a kind that I had never approached or heard tell of—totally unlike any known in the upper world.

Again I was startled by the sound of Ursilla's voice. This time she did not speak to me. She shaped odd, slurred, almost hissing sounds, which bore no relation to any words I knew. Nor were they a chant such as she had uttered on the stairs, but were uttered in a broken pattern, almost as if she spoke with one unseen, waited to be answered, then spoke again. There was no sound out of the dark to match what she said.

Instead, there came a chill wind that wreathed around our bodies, enwrapping us both as a giant, invisible hand might close upon us. The low wail of the wind was the voice of something that had never borne shape as we knew it.

There comes a point when one is dulled to fear. Or perhaps the place, with all its strangeness, laid some spell, so that fear could not break through to lodge in one's mind. I did not fear, nor now was I curious. I accepted all that lay here as a part of its difference, which was not of my world.

Ursilla's wand moved in her hand, back and forth, swinging from left to right. Now a brilliant fire shot from its point and touched something ahead that answered with a glow. Then there was an answering glow to the left, one to the right—an island of light lay before us.

So we came into a circle of radiance. For circle it was.
Tall monoliths of rock formed the place. Each was carven
into the likeness of a seated or enthroned being. Straightly
their bodies sat on blocks of stone, facing inward—save
that they had no faces!

Where features might have been wrought, there was
naught but an oval globe. Globe, I say, because they were
not stone; rather some other substance behind which light
moved and wove patterns. From the globes the light of
the place spread. Awakened by the beams of Ursilla's
wand, it lapped from one figure to the next, until all
showed blind but brilliant countenances.

Above the globes were ornate headdresses, each vary-
ing in detail from the next. Their bodies were human in
shape, but muffled in cloaks so that details were hidden.
Each had stretched forth a hand (I say hand, yet the
appendage was more like unto a claw so slender were the
"fingers"). And the hands held objects, again each differing. Here was a ball incised with patterns, there a wand
not too unlike those of the Wise Women, again there was
a flower, with petals widespread. But the one that Ursilla
faced had in its hand a man—small as a child's plaything,
drooping limply as if dead, or perhaps not yet called to
life. The sight of the carved human struck through my
dull acceptance of the place, disturbed whatever spell of
lethargy had been laid upon me. For it suggested that
men were but the playthings of the forces these faceless
ones represented, and that hint of slavery aroused protest
in me.

Ursilla knelt upon the floor. Not to do homage to the
figure before her, rather to set out the bundles, flasks and
boxes she had brought from her store. She seemed
oblivious to the glowing nonfaces, though I was not. I
liked them less and less.

In the very center of the circle was a brazier wrought
also of the stone. Ashes, heaped within it, suggested that

this was probably not the first time Ursilla might have used it for purposes of her own. That she played with something which was far better not to disturb was a belief now strengthening within me.

Not of the Shadow, not of the Power—what then composed the force lingering here? Something so old and elemental that it was beyond the boundaries of good or evil, existing first in a time when neither of them had been born to eternally war in the lands and hearts of men. To tap such a force—rash, indeed, would that be. Her own ambition had brought Ursilla to such a deed, which made my awe and dislike of her deepen to fear and hatred.

I wanted to be out and away. Still I was chained here as much as I was chained within the pard's body. To one glowing globe, then to the next I raised my eyes, only to look quickly away again. The light patterns, forming and dissolving, the colors changing from one hue to the next with hypnotic speed—one might be caught and held by such.

As I nervously paced around the circle, avoiding Ursilla, busy as a housewife in setting out her plunder from the cupboard, I thought I could hear (not with my ears, but my mind as the Were had spoken to me) a distant whispering as yet not loud enough to be understood.

Ursilla made certain selections from her store, went to the brazier into which she dribbled handfuls of dried and crushed herbs with care, almost as if each broken leaf must be counted. When the last had fallen, the Wise Woman brushed her palms across her robe, then for the first time raised her head to regard me.

"What will be done shall be well done." She spoke cryptically. "My Power guided me here many seasons ago. Then I searched out the most ancient of our rune rolls to read the riddle of this place. Before we were here—and *we* are old beyond the numbering of our years—others dwelt in Arvon. They served their own forces, wrought with Power such as we cannot imagine. Their time passed, but they left behind them wells of their force, strained and weakened, perhaps, but still greater than aught even the Voices or the Shadow can summon in the here and now.

"I have waited, I have learned—" Her voice swelled in a chant that was close to a cry of triumph. "I know what can be done here—if one uses the talent. Uses it as I shall use it!"

I think she recited her own thoughts aloud, rather than spoke to impress me. Her face appeared lighted by an inner fire so that her skin held some of the glow of those featureless faces that ringed us in.

"We must wait now," Ursilla continued. "This is not a thing easily done. The right hour must be set, those needful summoned to take part."

She went from the brazier back to her supplies. Searching among them she found a bag and loosed its drawstring, to draw out a brown cake that she broke in two. As she munched on half of it, she threw the other section to me.

"Eat!" she commanded.

I wanted little to do with her, but that I must keep my strength of body brought me to obey. I crushed the cake in one bite and gulped it down. Though the stuff was tasteless to my pard's reckoning, I knew the substance for journeycake, meant to sustain life for long periods of time when one did not have access to ordinary food.

"She will come soon." Ursilla rubbed her hands together. "The sending laid upon her shall draw her. Then we shall make a beginning—and what an ending shall come of it!"

She laid her forehead on her knees as she sat at the foot of the one that held the man plaything. Perhaps she slept, perhaps she was entranced. I lay down as far from her as I could get. To venture into the dark was useless, I knew that as well as if she had told me so. This place would hold me until her spells permitted my going. Nor did I, at that moment, dare to try to separate man from beast. There was here too much the taint of the Older Things that I mistrusted as I had nothing before in my life.

Perhaps, I too, slept—or fell under some spell that held me in a state near to sleep. I roused quickly from what seemed a period of unconsciousness, the length of which I did not know. Ursilla had arisen and was standing close to where I lay, facing outward.

Her attitude was one of waiting and I listened intently. There was a faint sound of footfalls, another soft swish, which might mark the passage of a woman's skirt across the ground. Both grew ever louder.

At last, into the circle of light, moved she who came, the Lady Heroise. Her face was drawn and haggard. Now she looked years older, older even than her mother. But it was what she bore in her hands, held out well before her as if she hated the touch of it and wanted to keep it from her body, that caught and held my full gaze.

The belt! The belt that had drawn me back to Car Do Prawn.

I uttered a growl I could not suppress at its sight. On my feet, I was ready—

Ursilla flung out one hand in my direction. It was a hurling gesture, yet she tossed nothing I could see. However, whatever she threw upon me in that moment now held me helpless where I stood.

My mother's gaze was fixed. She walked as one who is ensorcelled, drawn to some meeting during her sleep. When Ursilla reached to take the belt from her, she gave a start and looked about her wildly.

Her face was a mirror of fear. "Ursilla!" Her words slurred together in a swift babble. "Maughus—Eldris—they have gone mad! They broke into your chamber. Maughus ordered that all within it be destroyed. When the men would not obey him, he hurled it all from the windows of the Tower into the courtyard, then piled it together with his own hands and set torch to it.

"He had sword to slay Kethan on sight, as one dealing with the Shadow, and has sent a messenger to Car Do Yelt where there is said to be one favored by the Voices, urging him to come and cleanse the Keep. He—he is like one mad! Even kin-killing is not beyond him now."

Ursilla showed no agitation. "He has gained some night companions, Heroise. Not lightly does one threaten a Wise Woman."

The Lady Heroise shuddered. "You have driven him beyond the borders of fear. He fears no more, he only hates—and wants to kill."

"Let him rage, his time for such will be short," Ursilla said calmly. "Even if he finds the door leading hither, he will not be able to enter until I permit. There are guardians set to prevent such intrusion. Shiver not, woman —this is the hour toward which we have ever looked. You have thought to rule Car Do Prawn, I say that you shall rule a larger part of the land."

My mother wrung her hands, then wiped them up and down on the skirt of her robe, as if she wished to wipe so from them some taint that the belt had left on her flesh. She stared about her wildly as if she did not know where she was.

"Ursilla—the Magician! I have head the cards and the Magician lies in Kethan's Sixth House. It is a sign—a sign—"

Ursilla shrugged. "A sign of greatness to come. You have told me this before and I explained to you what such a reading may mean. It is foolish for you to claim more foretelling than you have. We have no need for such signs and portents, not here where another Power sleeps until we awaken it."

"I do not want—" my mother began. Tears gathered in her eyes, ran down her cheeks, dripped into her mouth as she spoke. "Please, Ursilla—this place—it frightens me!"

Ursilla shrugged. "You have left such qualms until too late, Lady. Now there is no retreating—"

My mother smeared her hands across her face, wiping away the tears as might a small child. Perhaps pity should have awakened in me at that sight, yet it did not. Close kin might we be, still at that moment, I felt nothing for her, when all she was and desired had brought us both to this.

Of How Ursilla Read the Smoke Runes and Sent Me to Do Her Bidding

Ursilla moved with the surety of one who knows well what must be done. She made a slow circuit of the seated ones, pausing for a moment before each to gaze fixedly into the flowing, ever-changing globe that served it for a face. So intent was her study that she might have been reading in the ceaseless flow of muted colors there a message each had for her. In the end, she once more faced the one that dangled the man-toy from its claw fingers.

Now she raised her voice, but not in any chant. She

brought out, from the front lacing of her robe, a small bone whistle that hung from a silver chain. This she put to her lips, drawing from it a thin, eerie piping that hurt my pard's ears until I could have roared my protest aloud, yet that I could not do.

Then—

From somewhere there came a faint and very faraway answer to the whistle. Maybe it was not distance that separated us, but rather time—or so the thought touched me. Three times did Ursilla sound that call, three times was she answered. Each answer grew stronger, as if what she so summoned drew closer.

She turned halfway about to point the tip of her wand at the brazier she had so carefully filled. From the wand came a burst of vivid fire, like a lightning flash, to bedazzle the eyes. That within the brazier was kindled and flared up. However, the flame did not last. Back it sank to smolder, and what followed were puffs of smoke.

Though the cold wind we had felt here earlier had long since died away, and there was no troubling of the air I could detect, the smoke streamed at a sharp angle toward the figure with the man-toy, wreathing it around until the bulk was nigh hidden except for the gleam of the featureless ball face. There the colors grew richer and stronger, their rippling changes swifter. I held my head lowered, fearing to allow my gaze to center there. For in me grew the idea that this might be the fashion in which this very ancient force could work upon its victims.

Ursilla allowed the whistle to drop from her lips, to hang upon her breast as the Moon Witch's crescent pendant lay—

The Moon Witch!

I was shaken by the conviction, even as memory presented me with a picture of her, that I must not think of her, nor of any who were of the Star Tower, not in this place! Could the influences Ursilla summoned so recklessly, reach far enough out when they were called to break the peace of that forest refuge? I did not know, but neither did I want my own unthinking action to provide any bridge.

Now Ursilla's thin body swayed from side to side, though her feet remained fixed in one position on the pavement. The smoke cloud swayed with her, sending out tendrils right and then left. They appeared to hang in the air for a moment, then clasp the figures on either side of the one she fronted.

In such a manner did the smoke spread to enclose them all, to wall us in. When the last gap was united, no more smoke came from the brazier. What had burned was now only a nearly consumed, dusty powder.

Now the globes were blazing. I heard my mother breathing in heavy gasps. Her fear was like a visible cloak, blowing out from her shoulders in some gale. Then—

There was no longer any sense of fear, or even of identity from her. When I turned my head to look, she stood blank-eyed. Yet her body also swayed in perfect time with Ursilla's. Whether the Lady Heroise willed or no, she was now a part of whatever the Wise Woman would do here.

But I was not. There was that within me which held stubbornly against this witchery. I knew who I was and whyfor I was here. Those facts I held in my mind, keeping my eyes from the glowing globes. Now I refused to watch directly either Ursilla or my mother, lest their absorption also entangle me.

Ursilla raised her wand, pointed out. This time no fire sprang from its tip. Instead, she moved the rod into the edge of the smoke as if she wielded some huge pen and was writing on the insubstantial surface with it. What she saw in answer to what she did, I had no way of knowing.

I would give quick glances at her actions, looking away again within the instant, for fear that I might be entrapped. To me all her gestures were meaningless.

Yet there was a force at work here. My skin tingled, a cold grew outward from my spine to seize my legs. I wanted to throw up my beast head and howl aloud my fear and awe. Elemental was the force. It might have been churned up from the age-old rock about us. That this energy had aught to do with my species was false. Nor could it, I believed, be channeled by such as Ursilla. I half expected to see the seated figures rise and trample upon the three of us for disturbing their quiet with our petty desires.

Ursilla's arm fell to her side, the point of her wand rapped against the floor. The smoke thinned more and more, drawing away from the figures, drifting in ragged wisps out into the darkness of the cavern. A short cry from my mother brought my attention.

She had sunk to her knees, her two hands hiding her face. Her body was visited by great shudders. But Ursilla still sood erect, facing the figure she had chosen to evoke, if that was what she had done here.

Slowly she turned. Her face was almost as masklike as those of the seated figures. Her eyes were wide open and never have I witnessed such a glow in any human eyes. Almost, one could believe that there was a massing of twisting colors behind them, even as there was behind the face-globes.

She spoke then and her voice was calm, with a remoteness of tone that I had never heard in any voice before.

"It is begun, well begun. Now is the time for you to play your part."

Her wand swept up, not pointing to the Lady Heroise, but rather to me. I was taken by surprise and had no defense ready.

There was no crackle of fire bursting from the rod this time. Instead what came was a command—a command and the knowledge to carry it out, implanted in my mind. Nor could I gainsay the order. Her desire ruled my body, both beast and Kethan.

"Go!"

Again she pointed with her wand. Not back in the direction from which we had come, but out past the figure she had paid homage to—into the darkness.

Within me, it was as if both Kethan and the pard now were locked into a third entity, with the order Ursilla had given in full control of my body and mind. It seemed as if Kethan watched what happened, as a man might look out from the window of a Keep cell.

Even as she ordered, so did I go. Out into the dark I sped, without even the wan glow of the wand light to show me any path. I did not need it. There was a sense of direction implanted in the order itself that drew me like a collar about my throat, the leash fastened thereto tugging me along.

Dark was the cavern, a velvety black that even a moonless night might not achieve. And it was very large, for though I ran hard, my paws spuring dust as I went, still there seemed no end to this journeying.

At last I came to what seemed the far end of the place, and there I slowed a little as I blundered blindly onto a ramp way that led upward. This time there was no stairway, only a series of ramps, each a fraction steeper than the one behind. The urgency laid upon me kept me at the best pace I could make under the circumstances, climbing, climbing through the dark.

However, the farther I withdrew from the strange place the lighter became the weight upon me. I could not escape the geas Ursilla had set upon me, no. I think it would have taken one well learned in sorcery to break that—if it *could* be broken, forged as it was from learning forgotten long ago. But behind the geas, I could think again, perhaps plan some way to bring Ursilla's plans to naught.

That I would come out in the Keep, or even near Car Do Prawn, I doubted. I believed that I would have little to fear from Maughus at this moment. But what I had to circumvent was what Ursilla's orders would have *me* do. I must reserve my strength against the time when I would face that action.

Up and up—how long had we been here? How long did it take to reach the living world? There was only the dark and the way before me, and to each I began to believe there was no end.

Then—far above as if it were a single star in the night, I sighted a wan, grayish glow. There was an end! Heartened by that sight, I again quickened pace, though my limbs were wearied with the strain set upon them, and my ribs ached with every panting breath I drew.

The gray spot was sharper, somewhat brighter. Yet it had none of the promise of sun or even daylight. All I dared hope was that it opened out on the surface. At last I drew my weary body up a slope, which was the sharpest of all, and came out—into twilight.

Around me, shutting off much of the view, were rounded mounds. From the sides of some of them protruded worn blocks of worked stone. I might be in some very old and forgotten temple or Keep. I turned my head to survey the door through which I had come. It was a dark hole in one of the mounds, with nothing to mark it of any importance.

However, the compulsion laid upon me gave me no time to study my surroundings further. Again my invisible leash jerked. There was that which I must do—a way to follow until I found what Ursilla must have to finish the sorcery she would need to buttress her desire.

There was a person—somewhere—Ursilla must have that one—I had no name, not even a mental picture. But the geas would lead me to the one. Then—that one must I bring back.

Just as the man within the pard had refused when Ursilla had cried "Kill!" and my enemy stood before me, so now did all that was me—both man and pard, prepare to fight this command. But not yet. Instinct (or something akin, which had come to me during my own struggles as a

Were) told me, warned me—do not waste your forces fighting until the proper time.

I padded swiftly through the coming night, turning this way, that—always guided by the geas, as if my nose sniffed out a plain trail. The land through which I moved was forest-edged. I recognized no part of it however, and I thought that I was farther east than I had ever been before.

The mounds were behind me now, trees closed in. The forest was very silent. I heard no stirrings of any other creatures. This portion of the land might be deserted by all life.

I came to a spring and drank thirstily, washing from my muzzle and throat the dust of that dark cavern. But I did not hunger or hurt. The thinnest sickle of the new moon arose. Seeing it gave me knowledge that we must have spent a far longer time in the cavern than I had judged.

It provided no light, but my pard's eyes probed the dark well, and I needed no guide. Twice I edged by places wherein there was the stink of the Shadow, like pools of corruption. I hated them so I snarled as I slunk past, wishing I could tear them utterly apart.

What dangers lay at their cores I did not guess, and I had neither time nor inclination to explore. However, I dreaded the fact that such appeared to be spreading in the forest.

It was not until I reached the river that I guessed where my quest was drawing me—back toward the Keep! Who there was my quarry? Maughus? Eldris? Even Thaney? I had no love for any of the three, but in the final moment that which was me would struggle in their defense. Or else I would die—though perhaps my body might live on.

As I crossed the river in bounds from one water-washed stone to the next, I began to believe that it was

not the Keep to which Ursilla had headed me, but elsewhere. Then I knew—

The Star Tower!

Had Ursilla guessed (or perhaps read from her spells)
that the ones therein had given me aid to escape her?
Was this her revenge?

I tried to fight, to control the pard's body. To no avail.
Though I snarled in fury at my own helplessness, still I
moved through the night, heading straight for those who
I would least harm. My horror at what Ursilla had done
to me was so great that had Maughus stood before me
in that moment with his sword, I would have leaped to
impale my body on the blade.

Now I strove to reach those ahead with some mind-
warning. The trick of mental contact I did not have, but
I could hope that part of their own defenses set by the
Power would pick up some troubling to alert them.

As sharp as the thrust of the sword I wished would
strike me down, there came an answer.

"We know."

The Were snow cat! As he had spoken with me before,
so was he in touch with me now.

"Kill!" I thought to him. Better that I lay dead than
Ursilla succeed in whatever deviltry she would do. All I
knew was that I must return with the one the Wise Woman
had selected. The rest of the peril I could guess.

"Come—"

That was not the snow cat. The woman of the Star
Tower spoke then. She must not let down her defenses—!

Feverishly, I tried to project my thoughts, let them see
the evil that rode with me to imperil their peace. How
much Power Ursilla might wield through me now I could
not judge. However, I feared that what she gathered in
the cavern was stronger and stranger than anything
known now on the surface of Arvon. And that the Star
Tower could defend itself against it, I feared, was futile.

Before me lay the garden clearing and the Star Tower. I breathed in the rich scent of the herbs. And I expected to see the haze of the protective wall about the points, the mist as I had seen it before. Perhaps that would hold even against the force Ursilla had aroused.

However, there was no haze. On the path before me stood three shadowy forms, as if to bid me welcome. I fought with my own body, struggled to stop well short of them. For now it was made plain to me whom I was sent to seek—

The Moon Witch!

"Kill me!" I thought again. There was no hope of self-preservation left now. Either I would die here and now, or such untold evil as I could not imagine would engulf this maid—perhaps the others, too, but certainly her.

None of the three shrank from me and the Wereman did not heed my frantic plea. I saw then they were garbed as they had been when they had backed me with their Power in Ursilla's Tower room. They held high their symbols of Power—the branch with its single green leaf, the rod interwoven with moonflowers, the sword. The latter—its blade should be aimed at my heart, my throat.

I snarled and growled, my fury rising. Why did they not heed me? I came to bring disaster upon them, yet they made no move.

The woman first extended her wand toward me. Perhaps she could aim a force through that—destroy me—

Instead there flowed into my churning thoughts and fears a soothing, as her herbs had soothed my torn skin when I lay under her tending. The urgency Ursilla had laid upon me as a goad, was muffled, muted—

"I am a danger—" I thought. Though I was not sure on my side of any contact, I hoped that the Wereman, at least, could read that warning.

"We know—we have seen."

His answer formed clearly in my mind. I longed to ask

how, but they must have their own ways of reading spells aimed at them.

"I must take—*her!*"

Again I gave warning. Surely they could understand by now that Ursilla's sorcery had left me no escape. Either I took the Moon Witch back into the buried cavern, or I would die. Of the two choices, the last was the better.

"Not so." Again came the Wereman's reply. "We have foreread through the water, through the stars, through the fire. Destiny is somehow entangled for us and you with us. We cannot right the scales until we face this sorceress of Car Do Prawn, that is the reading.

"There is ax time," he continued. "And there is sword time. They are the times of human man. There is wind time and Star times—which are the times of the Great Lords and the Voices. And there is Weretime and spell time—these last twain call and govern us."

I did not fully understand what he would say. But that our destiny was entwined amazed me, though I did not doubt his words. For if he were no Voice, yet that he governed Powers of his own was something I well knew. Now the woman's voice rang through my thoughts.

"Earth and Air, Fire and Water. By the Dawn of the East, the Moon White of the South, the Twilight of the West, the Black Midnight of the North, by yew, hawthorn, rowan, by the Law of Knowledge, the Law of Names, the Law of True Falsehoods, the Law of Balance —so do we move."

As her words sped through my mind, leaving nothing but wonder behind them, the Moon Witch advanced from the others, coming straight to me. She laid her hand upon my head as she had done the other time when she had bid me seek out the key of my enchantment. From her light touch more easement of my burden flowed.

"The moon is thin, but it lives," she said aloud. "It waxes, and so does that which arms me. What you would have me do shall be done. And I think that your sorceress shall not find the facing of what shall come easy."

Thus, when I turned my back upon the Star Tower, in truth I did not go alone, for the Moon Witch walked beside me. And behind came the woman, as surefooted and swift as the great snow cat that padded at her side. We crossed the river, heading back the way I had come, the same guide drawing me straight as a released arrow.

Yet the easement they had given me allowed a slower pace. We walked the night, we did not race through it. Now and again the Moon Witch's hand would brush my head. And each time she did so her touch lightened my heart, strengthened my hopes that what I brought back to Ursilla was not what she wanted, but what she deserved.

The false light of near dawn was about us when we came into the place of tumbled mounds. But when we were nigh to the dark hole of the cavern entrance, the woman cried out.

I turned swiftly to face her. She had halted, had her hand out before her, running it up and down in the air as if she laid her palm against some surface. There was naught there that I could see, and the Moon Witch and I were several paces past that point.

The snow cat reared on his hind legs and rested his huge paws on an invisible barrier. Growling, he extended his claws, raking them as if along a vertical surface.

My hardly won hope was smothered in an instant. I needed no words to tell me that there was a force field in existence here—one that admitted me and my victim, but not the two who would lend us their support.

I tried to retreat, to take with me the Moon Maid. For I mouthed some of the disk-strung strings of her skirt to pull her. However, just as the others could not come forward, so I could not return.

The forward pull on me was so strong that I knew I could not long withstand it. I would be drawn underground, forced to bring the Moon Witch with me. Better that the Wereman had done as I had begged and slain me out of hand. Destiny entwined or not, they could not reach me now, and I could not reach them.

Of How the Lady Heroise Told the Truth and I Confronted Ursilla

"Go!" The snow cat's command startled me. I was as one caught between two imperative orders, each of which dragged at me—in opposite directions.

"Go!" The Tower woman echoed him. "This is not a spell of might, but one worn thin by years, one we can break. However, if you linger, then she who awaits you shall know and perhaps send that to make this barrier the stronger."

I wanted to believe that it was the truth. But dared I? Only the Moon Witch's hand on my head once more, her face turned resolutely toward the hole of utter darkness, told me that if I could not accept the complete belief in the others' Power, she had. Fearless she appeared, only she did not realize—

Reluctantly I went forward, she matching pace with me.

"There is great dark here," I thought. "I am led, I do not know how—"

"Then I am led also," she returned. "For we shall be one now."

Thus together we entered the hole, descended warily the first of the ramps. I soon could not see her, even through my heightened cat senses, but her touch never left me.

Then—a dim glow moved beside me. Something not unlike the haze that enwreathed the Star Tower. It came from the disks that made her brief kilt, from the horned moon on her breast.

"There exists a great force here," she said then. "It awakens all that is in tune with Power." In her other hand she swung forward her flower-studded wand. I saw that each of the flowers, widely open, produced a wan circle of light. "Even though Mother Moon reaches not into the earth, yet her Power is fed here. Long ago there must have walked some in this way who knew the moon calls and used them."

That she was not alarmed awakened still more strongly my own fear for her. I tried to express the fear by voice, forgetting that I had only the gutterals of the cat to make myself heard. Again she must have read my thoughts.

"No, Kethan. I do not deny that this Wise Woman of yours has sorcery beyond my knowing. But also, I do not believe that she reckons that I, in turn, can summon some that may, in turn, be strange to her. I have been well taught.

"When I was still so young a child that my speech was not plain, I saw beyond the barriers of men. My mother, reading the fire and the water, knew that I had in me

talent, and one that differed from her own. However, that
is not a fact to be amazed at. For my mother is a Witch
of the Green Way and my father once was a Wererider."
She said that as proudly as one who recited a listing of
blood-kin heroes in some Keep.

"My mother, knowing that I would be a worker of
force, took me to the Fane of Neave. Those who serve
there weighed my talent and said that I would be a Moon
Drawer. Thus, when I was somewhat older, I went to
join those of Linark. There I learned much. From my
mother and my father still more when I returned to
Reeth. For long ago there was Moon Magic at Reeth
and the stirrings of it were still alive when my mother
and father discovered the Tower and took it for their
dwelling."

Her words came easily. She might have been speaking
to some friend as they walked across any open field. Still
we were going farther and farther into the depths of the
earth, to face a Power that I believed greater than my
race had ever tested before.

I had been right in my guess. The snow cat had been
a Wererider. But why was he not then at the Gray Towers?

"My mother," the girl beside me continued, perhaps
because again she had read my thought question, "was a
Bride of the Dales. Have you not heard that tale Kethan?
It is so famous a one that songsmiths have already
worked it into the Chronicles."

Yes, that I had heard. The Wereriders had been among
those exiled from Arvon when the struggle of the Elder
Lords came to an end. Far were they sentenced to
wander, and to be homeless, until there were certain
changes in the star readings. Then they might ask to
return.

South to the Dales they had gone. Later, when there
had come a war of men against men—long before I was
born—they had made a pact with the men of the Dales,
the ones who had taken over our deserted lands. They

served beside the Dalesmen, driving the invaders of High Hallack to the sea, or slaying them.

In exchange for their services, the Wereriders had stated a price, that when the war was done and High Hallack victorious, they would receive from the Dales Lords maids to be their brides.

Thus in the Year of the Unicorn, thirteen such maids were brought to the border of the Waste. They chose among the Wereriders and so came into Arvon and to the Gray Towers. But that there had been a Witch among them—that part of the tale was new to me.

"They did not know my mother was of Witch blood. She was taken as a child from overseas, found captive on a ship of the invaders and fostered by a Dales Lord. But the talent lay in her. That caused trouble among the Riders, for they feared to bring one of Power among them.

"They strove to lose her in the Other World, yet there she and my father fought a battle and won, so returning to their bodies here. However, thereafter, my father would not dwell in the Gray Towers, for he liked not what the Riders had done in their fear. So he and my mother found Reeth—or rather they were told of Reeth. Thus the Star Tower came to be our abiding place. Of Reeth we have made a place where the Green and the Brown Magic are entwined, to stand as a stronghold against the creep of the Shadow.

"But now Arvon is again troubled. There is talk of Gates about to open, exiles to return. Not all of them are like the Riders, willing to accept peace. Lately the Riders themselves have sent messengers to my father, saying the day comes when they shall be summoned to defend their lands. Not yet has he answered them fully. I think in him kin-ties pull one way, his old anger another. Until he settles that struggle within himself he cannot say he will do this or that. But Reeth's hold on him is, we hope—my mother and I—greater than one of memory—

since much of that was unhappy. Reeth has a place, so our
foreseeings show, an important place in Arvon. Long was
it forsaken, but now it lives, and, within it, the force of
that life grows!"

As she continued, I could almost see through the complete dark the rise of the Star Tower walls, smell the
scent of the herbs that made the garden around it. My
longing to be there once again was like a pain.

"Yes," she said, and I felt that she sensed the longing.
"Reeth is like a warm hand, to cup protectingly around
one. Still it is what we do that makes the hand endure."

My mind turned to what I now did and I was sickened.
I strove to halt my body, I fought against the compulsion
Ursilla had laid upon me. To play Ursilla's foul game,
with the Moon Witch as a part of it—no, that I could
not allow!

I snarled and spat. My limbs would not answer the
commands of Kethan—the pard was Ursilla's thing! Again
the Moon Witch's hand rested on my head. I could not
reassure her, yet she strove to reassure me! And she could
not possibly understand to where I took her, what might
await her there.

"Kethan." Her words took on the solemnity of a chant.
"My name—it is Aylinn, my mother is Gillan, my father,
Herrel."

It took a full instant out of time for me to realize what
she had done. By naming herself and the two from the
Tower, she had claimed a kind of kinship. For a name is
the inner core of a man when the Power is in use. And
to grant that knowledge to another is the fullest trust
one may bestow.

"You should not!" I protested.

"Ah, but I have!" There was something akin to laughter
in her reply. Not the horrible laughter of Ursilla's
triumph, but rather the joyful note one hears among
happy friends. The sound of it warmed me as no fire
had ever done. For, though many in Car Do Prawn could

claim me as kin, there had been none I could name in return as friend. Those of the Star Tower were as cup-companions and shield-mates.

"This is a long way," Aylinn commented, as one who was now a little shy and would speak of matters less close.

"I do not know how long," I returned.

While she had told me of herself I had not been aware of the crushing darkness. Now it wrapped us about as if to smother us in its heavy folds. I wished that I had counted the ramp ways when I had come up so I knew how far we needed now to descend. But then I had been driven by a single thought—to reach what Ursilla had sent me for.

Down and down. The glow of my companion's kilt and pendant remained alight but showed little beyond the portions of her own body against which they rested. Still, any light in this place brought with it a measure of comfort for those who were bred for the surface of the world and not its depths.

At last we reached the floor. I turned left, to head out into the center of the cavern, for it was my belief that the circle of globe-faced figures must form the center. Far ahead there was a faint speck of light in that direction.

The cord of force that had guided me back tightened. I thought Ursilla was aware we came, and I warned my companion of that fact.

"In truth she must know." Aylinn's answer was tranquil. "She already moves to meet us. However, Kethan, what she does not know is that Gillan and Herrel have broken the force barrier above and are now following."

How could she tell that?

Again the sensation of soft laughter. "Kethan, for purposes of the Power we have been one in minds and hearts several times over. Any part knows when the whole is near—"

I did not quite understand it. But her certainty again

raised my hopes. What Ursilla could do I dreaded because it was unknown. However, the confidence of my companion suggested that perhaps this time the Wise Woman would meet opponents she could not so easily defeat.

We were running now, I with the pard's leaps, as the strength of the bond jerked me on and on, Aylinn lightly, as she might have done across some woodland glade in utter freedom.

Thus we came to the figures. But there were others among them—Maughus! How had he won to this place? And the Lady Eldris! My cousin and my grandam stood statue-still. They might have been carven from the same stone as the seated ones. There was no sword in Maughus's hand, though one lay bare-bladed at his feet.

His face was a mask in which fear and anger were intermingled. But the one my grandam wore was of fear alone, though, when her eyes shifted now and then toward my mother, hatred shone there also.

Ursilla waited for us, her wand of Power outstretched as a fisherman might hold a pole by which he has hooked a catch he now draws to shore. Aylinn no longer moved beside me. When I glanced back, I saw her face in the light from the glowing globe-visages of the surrounding figures. It was serene, but set—another mask, save that this reflected no emotion, and her eyes were alive.

Her flower-enwreathed wand lay across her arm as if it were indeed only a sheaf of long-stemmed blooms she had gathered along the way. If Ursilla believed that the Moon Witch was truly part of her catch, she might well be surprised.

"Welcome, Kethan." Ursilla broke the silence of those within the circle. "You have done well—"

"And you—". She turned her glance from me to survey Aylinn from head to foot, then back again. There was startlement, quickly veiled in her eyes. Whatever she had expected, it was not to be confronted by the Moon Witch.

"So—" Her voice was a hiss as her wand moved, flicking back and forth as might a swordsman's blade before he engaged. Sparks flew from the rod as it swung. Then I saw Aylinn smile, not in victory, or in mockery, but openly, as a child would do.

"You have called, Wise Woman. I have come. What would you have of me?"

My mother wavered from where she stood on the other side of the brazier—her face mirrored open amazement.

"Who—are—you?" She breathed as might a nearly spent runner and pressed her hands against her breast as if to ease the pain.

"I am she who the Wise Woman has summoned," Aylinn returned.

The eyes of all were centered on her. Her bearing was as proud as my mother's when she was wrapped in her finest feasting robes.

"No!" The Lady Heroise retreated step by step as Aylinn advanced. My mother might be facing some wraith of the Shadow, which had intruded in this place. Her astonishment had changed to what was manifestly fear. Now, with a visible effort, she turned her gaze from Aylinn to Ursilla. Her voice rose shrilly. "You have brought the wrong—"

"Not so!" Ursilla interrupted. She lowered her wand, though still held it with the point toward Aylinn, who did not seem to notice it at all.

"The spell does not fail, not with the force of the ancients behind it," the Wise Woman continued. "Which means—"

My mother lurched forward as one so stricken she could not keep her feet without support. Her groping hand fell upon Ursilla's shoulder.

"This cannot be!" Her protest now was near a scream.

"Do you think I know not our Clan blood? We have no talent beyond the lesser. This is one possessing Power!"

I listened completely bewildered. There was something between my mother and the Wise Woman, something that made my mother completely oblivious of all else.

"You did not ask concerning the father." Ursilla's thin lips stretched in a grin akin to the grimace of a fleshless skull. "Did you know his blood-kin?"

My mother dropped her grasp on Ursilla and cowered away. She beat her rolled fists together. "No! What did you then summon to my bed? What have I bred?"

Ursilla laughed, the same terrible laughter I had heard when she promised to make Maughus rue his violence.

"Seemingly better than you thought, my Lady. As for the breed of your mate—you did not care. It was the child who mattered." Now the hand that did not hold the wand made a sign in the air, which flamed orange.

Bewildered, I looked from one to the other. The secret they had held between them so long was first understood by Maughus. His body rocked a little as if he tried to move and could not. But there was a wild light of triumph on his face.

"So—that was what you wrought!" he spat at the two before him. "Now it comes clear to me. You went to Gunnora to bear your heir, my Lady. There all your charms failed you, for you bore a daughter instead of a son! Where got you then this Shadow-bred mongrel?" He looked to me with a death wish in his eyes.

In that moment, he had ripped wide open all the past, made many things clear to me. Yes, I could see plainly what had chanced—that the Lady Heroise and Ursilla, their ambitious plans ruined by the birth of a daughter instead of a son, could be tempted to exchange children. If Ursilla had now laid a spell to bring the missing daughter hither (and that I could believe), then Aylinn was that daughter. But who was I?

"Be silent!" Ursilla swung around, pointed the tip of

her wand at Maughus. His jaws clamped shut, his face reddened with anger, yet he could not utter another word.

"We have lost nothing," Ursilla stated firmly. "Why think you I have called—*her?*" She gestured toward Aylinn. "As long as she exists she is a threat. The more so, I now reckon, because she is what she is. Therefore, we shall rid ourselves of the threat. And"—she laughed that vile laugh—"in the ridding, we shall bind to us your dutiful son by such ties as he can never break and rid ourselves also of this loud-tongued fool." It was at Maughus that she nodded then.

My mother shrank yet farther away. She watched Ursilla with the look of one held entranced. But the Lady Eldris screamed, her voice awakening strange and spine-chilling echoes from out of the earth.

Ursilla reached within the inner pocket of her skirt. When she withdrew her hand, I saw what she held, all coiled together—the belt that anchored me to her will. She shook it loose. Where the hawk had torn it asunder it was mended.

In that moment, before she turned upon me the full force of her command, I made my move. Man—man! My will caught and held upon that one desire. All the energy I summoned, all I could find in either man or pard, that did I draw upon.

I stood Kethan. The beast was gone.

Again the Lady Eldris screamed. This time Lady Heroise echoed her cry. Beyond Ursilla I saw Aylinn give a small nod. She held her beflowered rod in my direction. Through that, I believed, had come an additional surge of energy to my aid.

Ursilla did not seem disconcerted by my transformation. She might even have been expecting some such move on my behalf. This made me wary. I stooped, caught up the sword that had fallen at Maughus's feet. He himself was fighting whatever force held him, but his fight was in vain.

Ursilla raised her wand. I wondered if I could knock it from her hand with the length of steel I now held. Iron is a remedy against some forms of sorcery. Though would Ursilla have allowed me to arm myself so had she had any fear of that? I thought not.

However, she did not aim the wand at me, but again at the brazier. For the first time I noticed that it was once more filled and ready to be fired. A beam struck into its contents, smoke began to rise and this time, with it, flame tongues.

The Wise Woman again laughed. "Well armed you are now, Kethan, for what must be done. This is no place of the Shadow as we know it in these lesser days. But there are forces that will gather here to drink new-spilled blood. And, having so been fed, they will then be amiable to command—for a space. Therefore—they shall have their feast!"

Now the wand was pointed toward me at heart level.

"Kill," she said calmly, as if she uttered an order no different from any one might give a servant in hall or stable.

My arm rose, though I fought it with all my will, even as I had fought to be a man not a pard moments earlier. Also, I willed my tight grip upon the sword to loosen, to let it fall once more into the scuffed-up dust of centuries.

My struggle was as fierce as Maughus's had been, yet I took one step forward, then a second. My sword was pointing now, straight at Aylinn's white body.

No! I stopped, swayed. Let me be beast for all my days then! This I would not do! Let Ursilla blast me with her sorcery, with all the menace that lurked in this place. Let her kill my body—kill the essence of me that dwelt within that body. *This* I would not do!

I tottered back and forth, the point of the sword wavering up and down as Ursilla's will vied with mine for control.

"Run!" I shouted, and it was echoed out and out—
"Run—run—run—"

Still Aylinn stood where she was. Her eyes held mine.
I could not understand why she did not flee. Had Ursilla,
in some way, woven about her the same stass-spell as held
Maughus and his grandam?

"Kill!" Ursilla's command was shriller. I could feel the
anger in it.

I summoned the last of my own will—and held fast.

Then—

Pain such as I had never known before racked my
body. I cried out.

Ursilla held the belt over the flames in the brazier,
feeding the length of the strap to them little by little. As
the fire licked at fur and hide, so did it also eat upon
my flesh.

"Kill," she cried. "Kill or die in torment!"

The victory might well be hers! I could not hold long
my concentrated will as the agony ate into my mind and
body. But while I could—that I would.

Of Sorcery Wrought and Unwrought and How We Learn Our Destiny

Through a red mist of pain I saw Aylinn lift her flower wand in my direction. There followed an instant or two of relief from torment. Only it did not hold. Again the flames engulfed me as they avidly licked the belt Ursilla dangled into their reach.

Then, in spite of my torture, I saw the belt begin to writhe in Ursilla's hold, even as a living thing might fight for freedom. With a mighty jerk, it tore loose from her fingers and moved through the air. A hand arose, caught it.

Gasping, I stood free of the torment of those last moments. The belt lay in the hands of her whom Aylinn had named Gillan and Green Witch. Beside her crouched the snow cat, eyes aglare in the reflection of the brazier fire. Ursilla tottered. The force of the pull that had brought the belt out of her grasp had upset her not only bodily, but threatened her control of the force she had summoned.

She stared first, unbelievingly, at her empty hand, then raised her head slowly and looked at the two who stood just without the circle of the seated ones. No shadows of the dark concealed them. Perhaps the light, which made them so plain to our eyes, came from the Power, as well as the illumination generated within the circle.

I saw Ursilla's face change. No years had drawn the flesh from her bones, but, in the few moments she confronted the two, age settled deep upon her, so that her coif framed a face that was close to a skull's visage.

"Who—are—you—?" Her words grated forth rustily. She might have been speaking against her will.

"Those summoned—" the Green Witch replied. "Did you believe, Wise Woman, you might call one of kin, without others also coming?"

"Kin!" Ursilla was recovering from the shock that confrontation had caused her. She threw back her head, a cackle of hideous laughter loud in this place. "Claim you this one"—she pointed to Aylinn—"as kin? You are wrong, woman! She is no blood of your blood. You and your furred lord did not have the fashioning of her! If you would see the child you truly bore—look to this fool!" Now her pointing finger moved to me.

"So we have heard—" Gillan showed no surprise. "There has been free talk among you and we have ears. Son—" she looked past Ursilla straight at me. "Take what is yours!"

Through the air she tossed the belt and I caught it. It came to my hand as neatly as it had gone to hers earlier. I made haste to fasten about me the singed belt but, as my fingers caressed it, I could not now discover any signs of fire damage upon it.

Ursilla snarled as a beast would snarl. Her wand swept up as if to ward off an attack. But I had already locked the jargoon buckle. The sword was in my hand. My own gaze was for Aylinn. What did it mean to her to have this old truth now bared? She who was one with Gillan and Herrel—

But—still she was one with them! I knew it as I looked upon her, for I could sense the strong Power that united them. Daughter of their bodies she might not have been, but daughter of their hearts and minds, that she truly was. She showed no surprise, her serenity remained. It belonged to one secure in who and what she was.

"Did you think, Wise Woman," Gillan asked, "that one could pass through the truth of Neave's own Fane and not learn even what sorcery strives to hide? This is our child by the will of *those* far greater than we ever hope to know—"

As I looked upon them, the Green Witch who was my mother, the Were who had fathered me, and Aylinn who was their chosen child, I could understand the justice of their choice. In me there was a cold desolation growing. Not from fear, but from the pressure of the loneliness I had known all my life, but that now was given meaning and completion.

I was no heir to Car Do Prawn. Maughus would have what he had always sought. Now I could be no tool for Ursilla's shaping either, since the truth was known. I was—apart and alone.

The retreat into self was my mistake. For Ursilla attacked. Her wand flashed up, its tip pointing at Aylinn. Fire burst, enwreathed my Moon Witch, hid her from sight. I heard a cry from out of the fire.

Then I leaped into flames that curled about me, caused a moment of raw agony. My lunge brought me to Aylinn.

I threw out my left arm to bear her back, away from the dancing tongues of flame.

We were together in a circle of fire, fire that burned not orange and red, but with hues a deeper, deadly color—the purple of the Shadow. We could not retreat farther, for our backs were against the rigid knees of the seated figure, about which the purple wall of shifting fire crept closer.

The Moon Witch held her staff against her breast. I could feel the rhythm of a chant throughout her body, though she did not open her lips. As she had done for me, so I tried in turn to do for her—to give her my strength to serve her purpose.

Then I moved swiftly, dropping the useless sword, catching her by her slender waist to toss her up upon the lap of the stone one. There was room there for her above the flames. Perhaps, before they could reach her, Gillan and Herrel might evoke an answer to the horror Ursilla had wrought.

Through the ever narrowing, creeping advance of the fire I could see the others. Ursilla worked feverishly, drawing about her feet with the tip of her wand another circle to enclose her, and the brazier. She threw something from the breast of her robe into the stone cup. More smoke arose to hide her. But her chanting I could hear—the hissing, slurred words to evoke the unknown sorcery of this place. Through the smoke I heard, a moment later, the shrill note of the bone whistle—a frantic summons.

"Kethan—up!" It was Aylinn's voice. She had curled up in her strange place of refuge and now reached toward me. But there was no room. And the purple flames gave off that which made my breath strangle in my throat, so that I choked and retched, as if all the evils of the world poured from within in a foul fog.

"Up!" Aylinn clawed at my shoulder. Her nails left red lines on my skin. I could feel the force of her will also, drawing me in the same way the spell Ursilla had laid had drawn me, first to her and then back to this cursed place.

Somehow her will did bring me up, so we huddled together on the lap of the seated one. It was not the figure that held the limp man-toy, for which I was dimly grateful. In its claw hand was a half-open flower. Now I saw Aylinn put forth her own hand to run fingertips across the stone petals, even as she might touch one of her moon-flowers.

She no longer was tense with the will to power which had been in her when first the fire ringed me round. Rather she waited—though for what event or signal, I did not know.

Ursilla's protective circle touched upon the base of the seated one with the man-toy. Now smoke whirled out in thick coils to enclose it along with Ursilla herself. I waited for more to flow around the circle, engulfing one of the faceless beings and then the next as it had done before. However, this time the puffs of smoke remained stationary. Through the upper reaches we could see, faintly, the flow of the globe face above us. In it colors spun with increasing force, growing ever darker.

The flames crept now to the foot of the statue on which we had taken refuge. It appeared to me that the fire burned with anger, if that can be said of fire, lashing out with many tongues in an attempt to reach us. Yet the highest flames were well below us.

For a moment (Though how long might that last?) we seemed safe. I gazed eagerly beyond the flames to see what chanced with the others. Ursilla remained hidden in her smoke veil. The three from the Keep huddled together, their eyes wide with fear. Whatever spell Ursilla had put upon Maughus was slowly passing. The Lady Eldris clung to him. He had freed one arm and raised it before them both. Though he was weaponless, his gesture was one of defense. Beyond them, near their feet, crouched the Lady Heroise. All her arrogance had ebbed. She did not any longer even weep as she had when she had come at Ursilla's bidding. Her face was blanched with fear, her staring eyes fixed upon the smoke cloud that concealed the Wise Woman. It was that, which drew all their attention. None looked at us above the flames.

There was good reason for that. Even the most insensitive of living creatures, one with no vestige of talent, would certainly have been aware of the forces collecting in that long-forgotten shrine (if shrine it was). Ursilla had thrown open some Gate—

One of the *Gates* of legend? Aylinn's head turned against my shoulder as that thought slipped into my mind. I read the wonder in her eyes.

We, who were born after the great struggle between the Powers of Arvon, knew only through legends what had occurred in the dim years of long ago. We had Chronicles that spoke often of the Gates and what could be summoned through them. (It was far harder to expel such aliens back through the uncanny openings in the skin of our world.)

But of the nature of the Gates themselves, or the keys that opened them, or where they might be situated, that knowledge was never made plain in the tales. Such was forbidden, shunned by all who dwelt in the Power—unless the Shadow now meddled in some way; for a check upon these of the Greater Dark was ever hard to keep.

It was well within reason, I believed, that this place could mark one Gate. And, if Ursilla, in her madness, threw it open—

Where were the two from the Tower? I had been so bemused, first by Aylinn's great danger, and then by the sorcery of the Wise Woman, I had almost forgotten them. Now I shifted as well as I could in the small cramped space of our refuge trying to sight them. However, the bulk of the figure, on which we sheltered, cut them from view. Aylinn's hand closed on mine.

Her flowered wand shifted in her other hand, pointed

toward the flower carved in the figure's hold. She tilted the rod carefully so that its tip rested in the heart of the stone flower.

"Give me," she said in a voice so low it could not have reached beyond my own ears, "give me all you have to give—kinsman!"

She did not glance toward me, rather fastened her full concentration upon the flower and the wand tip. A moment later, I knew that she had now become a channel for force, some of it raised by her own calling, some drawn from me. Though I was not practiced in such matters, I strove, as I had to separate man and beast, to release to her what small aid I could give.

So intense was my desire, my whole world narrowed to the small point where wand touched the carven flower. I could feel the energy going out of me, caught up by Aylinn, refined, strengthened, interwoven with what she had to give in turn. Then only did it flow down her wand.

Brighter blazed the moonflowers, the pure white radiance clear and clean above the sullen purple of the flames that still strove to consume us. The wand changed to a shaft of moon fire, eye-hurting in its brilliance.

Still Aylinn called upon me, still I gave freely, not reckoning any future cost.

Now, where the point of the wand touched, there showed a pale circle of fire. That, too, grew, brightened, spread out and up, to make the petals of stone resemble those of the moonflowers, as if the rock carving was transformed by our force of desire into a living thing.

I was dimly aware, even through my concentration, of something else. There was a change in the figure where we sheltered. Vibration ran through the substance of the shrouded body, not the vibration of breath, or heartbeat—but—akin to that!

I dared not allow myself to think of anything but what Aylinn would do now. I willed away suspicion of such change.

The flower was fully alight, to the very tips of its petals, not as purely bright as the moon blooms, rather silver instead. From the petal tips broke thin spirals of radiance, until what we could see, in truth, was not just the stone flower, but a much greater and more wonderful bloom sketched in the air about it.

Slowly the stone petals began to open further, folding back, as might those of a bud in full warmth of day. The other radiant petals, which the first guarded as a core, did likewise.

Out of the core emerged a sliver of silver light, another, more. I had seen field flowers, after blooming, scatter seeds that bore tufts of stuff upon them to aid their wind flight. Out and out flew these bits of light. Some vanished into Ursilla's smoke wall, some dropped sooner into the purple of the flames at our feet.

Aylinn raised her wand. She looked up and around over her shoulder, seeming to seek out the globe face that hung above us. The drain of energy had ceased. I felt too weakened to move. Yet, somehow, I forced myself to do as she had done.

There was still the ceaseless roll and swell of color captured within the oval. But—there was something else!

Had I seen it? Or had my imagination only for a moment made me think that I perceived eyes marked there, eyes that regarded me as if from a very great distance—eyes to which I meant little or nothing, eyes drowsy from sleep? I am not sure, and yet I believed that I did see this.

If such eyes did look upon us, they were quickly gone again. In Aylinn's hand her wand grew dark and drab. From its length the moonflowers withered, falling in seared bits. The stone flower and the radiance around it were gone. Where the seedlings (if seedlings the splinters of light had been) had fallen, there had been other results.

Of those that had met our prisoning flames, we could see no remains, but their passing was marked. For in certain places the circle of fire was quenched, leaving openings that no outward surge of fire could cross and close.

Also, in Ursilla's wall of concealing smoke, other light seedlings had torn wide windows. Through these we could look upon what happened as she called upon all she had learned to serve her in this time and place.

Now I could see that Gillan and Herrel had moved forward, to one of the windows in the smoke. The snow cat crouched low. Pard memory tightened my own muscles as the black tip of the silver-white tail quivered.

He leaped—threading through the window in the smoke expertly. Behind him, Gillan thrust forward with her leaf-tipped rod, aimed at Ursilla's head.

The Wise Woman had been standing with head flung back, her eyes shut, pouring from her mouth the stream of hissing, slurring calls. Now her head rocked forward as if dealt a shock. Her words, if words they were, were choked for a breath or so. At that moment, her incantation hesitated, the snow cat swung out a mighty paw in a blow such as few even of that great breed might hope to equal.

Claws raked and then caught. The brazier was over-balanced and fell. Out of its hollow spewed the burning stuff Ursilla must have mixed with such care. There was no more smoke arising from the scattered bits, quickly fading to ashes. The cloud of smoke, already in the air, began to fade.

But—

A cry arose in my own throat, echoed hoarsely from the dark. For the seated figure near Ursilla had—moved!

From its claw hand the man-toy fell limply, tossed aside as something now without value. But the claws hovered above the snow cat, closing in. I heard a Were-roar of defiance. Saw Ursilla's mouth stretch over sounds that seemed to distort her human lips. She lashed out at the cat, and he retreated before her wand as she drove him back under the slowly descending hand.

What could be done? Aylinn cried from beside me. I could not listen coherently to what she said. Rather I concentrated upon what I must do.

Gillan's leaf point quivered now. The wand to which it was fastened wavered back and forth. Her face was drawn by fear, not for herself, but for Herrel.

Then—not knowing I had made the descent—I was on the pavement. My fingers closed about the hilt of the sword I had dropped at the foot of the figure. This in hand, I staggered forward, forcing my drained body to do my will.

The snow cat had easily made the leap through the opening in the smoke. But the wall, save for that, was still intact: I had no time to hunt another doorway, nor did I have the strength to raise myself through the one that existed. I had only the sword—and to some sorcery iron was a deadly thing.

I drew on all the energy still in me, raised my arm shoulder high. Then I hurled the blade as I might have a spear.

Through the window in the smoke it carried. I had had such a short time in which to aim. And my weakness betrayed me. The point did not strike at Ursilla. Instead, it clattered feebly against her wand.

There was a brilliant flash of light, so great as to half-blind me. I threw up my arm to shield my eyes. So—I had failed!

"Kethan!"

Aylinn's hands were upon my shoulders. I knew her touch even though I could not see her.

I blinked, perceiving only a haze ahead, one shot through with color. Through it, in some strange fashion, padded on four feet an indistinct animal shape. The snow cat!

Gillan closed in upon my left, even as the cat reached

us. I blinked again, rubbed my eyes, hoping to clear away the fog born from the flash.

Now the last of the smoke was whirled away by a wind that arose out of nowhere. Crouched against the feet of the figure who had answered her spell-call was the Wise Woman.

By her feet lay the sword, its blade half melted, blackened. Of her wand there was no sign at all.

Ursilla was the focus of that wind. Under its buffeting, she cowered close to the pavement—and— She was—

She was gone! There was a length of cloth that had been her coif, a tangle of robe. But she was gone. Over where she had crouched hung the empty claw hand that had reached for a new toy to hold throughout the centuries.

"Her power"— Gillan's voice reached me dimly through the wind that still wailed— "her power was broken and then recoiled! She is—finished!"

"So be it!"

That was another voice, one I knew. Maughus moved away from the two women, watched us with eyes in which there was little of sanity left.

"If you think to take Car Do Prawn—" All that had happened appeared to mean nothing to him, his own cause was all that mattered. And he spoke thus to Aylinn.

She laughed. "What want I of your Keep?" She moved closer to Gillan. "I want no part of any heritage. I have my own place."

"You—" He swung now upon me. "*You* have no claim—"

"Nor want one," I told him. There was a vast weariness about me. "To you goes Car Do Prawn, Maughus. No man shall now gainsay your right."

He eyed me doubtfully. Perhaps he could not believe that I would not do as he might have done in my place, fight for the Keep. But to me, Car Do Prawn now seemed as far removed as a star, and far less desirable.

"Yes, Lord Maughus, to you Car Do Prawn—"

We all turned in startlement. There stood another, beyond the circle of the seated ones. Now he came briskly into the waning light. As he passed the place where some of the purple flames still danced fitfully, he waved his hand. They disappeared.

"Ibycus—" I was tired beyond the power to wonder what had brought the trader hither to this place and at this hour.

He bowed. "Just so, Kethan. I see that you have made excellent use of your gift—"

My hand fell to the belt. Part of me wanted to strip it off—hurl it from me. The other part forbade. Beast I might be again when there came a need, but now Kethan would ever control the pard.

He nodded. I knew he could read my thoughts as easily as if they were runes set out on some roll.

"Very true." Now he turned his head to look upon Gillan, and, behind her, Herrel, who once more stood a man.

I saw them both suddenly make the same gesture of respect, one I had seen used only from Keep Lord to a messenger of the Voices.

"You think we may have played some ill tricks, Lady?" Ibycus asked Gillan.

She hesitated. "I think rather there was meant to be a meaning to all of this that the players in your act did not know."

"You are entirely right. Ursilla would provide her tool, the Lady Heroise, with an heir—for her own purposes. Her efforts in that direction evoked the knowledge of one to whom is entrusted the duty of keeping the balance of power here in Arvon. Thus we made use of her ambition in order to temper those who are to stand firm in times to come. With you, Lady Gillan, Aylinn became the person she was meant to be. In Car Do Prawn, had Ursilla not played her own game, this maid would never have learned the depth and height of her own powers. While Kethan"—now he smiled at me—"was tested as a sword is tested by a smith, proving that he had the strength desired. And the last venture—within this you four have woven well a pattern that will hold—"

Herrel spoke as Ibycus paused. "I read in your words hints beyond hints, Messenger. Do we now venture once more into battle?"

"So much we can read, but that foreknowledge is limited. Your Werekin, with their Dale brides, have forged a new race. These two"—he gestured to Aylinn and then to me—"are also to be counted of that heritage. We have been informed that this is of importance, the whyfor will come to be discovered in time. Now—" He stood with his hands on his hips as his eyes studied each of us in turn. "This is no place for those of Arvon. Old and old it is, and best forgotten. Out—"

With his forefinger he pointed swiftly to Maughus, to the Lady Eldris, to Heroise. And—they were gone!

Us, he did not so indicate separately. But a wave of a hand included us four together. There was a breath of cold and darkness, then—

We stood with the sun of midmorning warm upon us. The other three watched me with an inner warmth, greater than any sun glow could ever be.

"Welcome home, Kethan!" said my father, as Aylinn drew me forward to walk down the door path of the garden.